From Fracas To Fame

War has become illegal, but "fracases," a highly controlled form of warfare similar to tournaments, are used as a means of entertaining the people and settling conglomerate disputes.

The latest fracas, however, was a madhouse. General Stonewall Cogswell lost all of his field officers, and Joe Mauser, a mercenary, and Max, his sidekick, were trapped behind enemy lines.

"What's in this fracas for you, Joe?" Max asked as the shells blasted around them.

"When you have been involved in the fracases as long as I have," Joe told him, "you become a celebrity. The fracas-buffs follow everything you do."

"Sounds awful," Max said.

"In some respects, it is," Joe admitted. "But you can't brush them off. Ultimately, the fracas-buffs help you to get a promotion in rank or a bounce up in caste level..."

Also by MACK REYNOLDS

Of Godlike Power
The Cosmic Eye
Trample an Empire Down
Brain World

THE
Fracas Factor

Mack Reynolds

A LEISURE BOOK

Published by

Nordon Publications, Inc.
Two Park Avenue
New York, N.Y. 10016

Copyright © 1978 by Nordon Publications, Inc.

This is the third of the "Joe Mauser, Mercenary," novels. The sequence of all four is: *Mercenary, Frigid Fracas, The Fracas Factor,* and *Sweet Dreams, Sweet Princes.* All the other novels have already appeared.

This country, with its institutions, belongs to the people who inhabit it. Whenever they shall grow weary of the existing government, they can exercise their constitutional right of amending it, or their revolutionary right to dismember or overthrow it.

Abraham Lincoln
First Inaugural Address

Chapter One

Joe Mauser was in the dill. The former major of mercenaries had been in the dill many a time in combat when the situation had pickled. But he wasn't in combat now. He was being stalked by five men who were obviously professional assassins, and he was inadequately armed. On top of that, he had an inexperienced companion to take care of, and little Max Mainz, being city-bred, was not only weaponless but wasn't used to this desert terrain.

It was Joe's own fault for getting off the main road. He had wanted to show Max the Guanajuato Military Reservation, where, more than ten years earlier, he had fought one of his most bloody fracases, the one between the two petroleum corporations, Pemex and Texas oil.

It had started in Frank Hodgson's office in the Octagon. The secret revolutionary head, who had infiltrated the government of the United States of the Americas to the point that he was now the assistant, and power behind the throne, of the Director of the North American Bureau of Investigation, had picked Joe as a courier.

Hodgson was a tall man who carried himself in a strange manner, one shoulder held considerably lower than the other to the point that Joe, when he had first met the other, thought it might be the result of a wound. But no, the bureaucrat had obviously never been a soldier. He had a heavy office pallor, the complexion of the man who seldom gets into the sun, seldom exercises. He affected an air of languor, obviously assumed and artificial, his bright, usually darting, eyes belying the affectation.

7

On this occasion, he'd had Joe Mauser summoned, and sat for a moment, crossing his legs and dragging an aged briar from a side pocket. He had a pound tin of pipe tobacco on his desk and loaded up while Joe took a seat.

He said, "You speak Spanish, don't you, Joe?"

"That's right."

Hodgson frowned at him, over the bowl of his pipe, even as he lit it. He said, "Where in the name of Zen did you ever learn Spanish? From your dossier, you were born a Lower, and, I assume, had all of the lack of educational opportunities that implies."

Joe nodded acceptance of that. "I always made a point when I was in the hospital of studying, rather than reading fiction or watching telly. You'd be surprised how much intensive study you can get in when you're laid up with a belly wound, or whatever, for a few months. Then I've fought a few times on the Chihuahua and Guanajuato Reservations in what they used to call Mexico, and once on the Honduras Reservation at San Pedro Sula. Gave me an opportunity to brush up my accent."

Hodgson said, letting smoke drool from his nostrils, "Wizard. I assume that Señor Zavala speaks Amer-English, but it won't hurt for you to have Spanish."

"Zavala?"

"Señor Jesus Zavala, in Mexico City."

"In Spanish, that's pronounced *Hey-Zeus*. Not the way we pronounce Jesus," Jose said. "What about him?"

"He's a new contact. Potentially influencing quite a few people of the type we need to swing that part of the country over to our way of thinking. We want somebody to size him up, give him the complete message, and begin whatever steps seem called for."

Joe frowned and gestured at the telly-phone on the

other's desk. "Why don't you just phone him?"

Frank Hodgson sighed. "Joe, I sometimes fear that you'll never get the hang of conspiracy. Any phone can be tapped—even mine. So far, Phil Holland and I have maintained our positions only by taking infinite pains to avoid exposure. We never discuss anyting pertaining to our underground organization over any public system of communications."

"Lesson learned," Joe said. "I'll take the rocket shuttle to Mexico City tomorrow."

Hodgson blew smoke through his nostrils again and shook his head. "No."

Joe looked at him.

The bureaucrat said, "If you utilize your credit card to buy passage on either an airline or in the vacuum-tube transport system, it will be recorded in the computer data banks and the time may come when somebody might wonder why Joe Mauser had cause to go to Mexico City."

"This is getting real cloak and dagger, Joe said. Should I take Max Mainz with me?"

"Why?"

"For the experience," Joe told him. "He showed up well in that set-to we had in Budapest with the Sovs."

"All right, take him along. By the way, we're making arrangements to bounce him from Low-Lower to Mid-Lower. And we're issuing him some Variable Basic Common Stock so he'll be able to increase his standard of living."

Joe scowled. "Mid-Lower? That's still pretty far down on the totem pole. Why don't you make him a Low-Middle?"

The bureaucrat relit his pipe and dropped the old fashioned kitchen match into an ashtray. He shook his head and said, "Because we need more members who

9

can communicate with the Lowers. Our ranks are composed too largely of Upper caste with a sprinkling of middles and an even smaller sprinkling of Lowers. If this socioeconomic change we advocate is ever to come off, the ending of Peoples Capitalism and the Ultra-Welfare State, we're going to have to be able to attract the Lowers. Zen knows, they compose ninety percent of the population. At any rate, you've got a car, Joe. Drive down. Get Señor Zavala's address from Miss Mikhail. Report back to me when you return."

It was in the way of being a dismissal. Frank Hodgson was one of the busiest men in Greater Washington.

"Got it," Joe said, coming to his feet. He supposed that was one of the reasons Hodgson had chosen him for the job. Joe owned his own sports hovercar in an age when few people owned cars. It was much simpler to rent one when needed, or use the ultra-efficient vacuum-tube transport system. There would be no record of Joe Mauser's trip to Mexico City in his own vehicle. Fresh power packs would allow him to drive all the way through, all the way back, without using his credit card. He and Max would have to sleep out at night and take food along with them. He assumed that Zavala could put them up one way or the other in Mexico City; otherwise, they could camp out. It was no hardship for old pro Military Category Joe Mauser. There would be no record of him going to the city of Montezuma.

They crossed the Rio Grande at McAllen to Reynosa and headed in the direction of Monterrey, even now still one of the most objectionably industrialized cities in North America, but Joe turned off at the town of China and headed southwest to Montemorelos and then down to Linares where he turned right.

This was one of the few drives in northern Mexico

that had any charm. He'd been over it before. In fact, he'd had one of the most exciting bed companions he had ever known in Linares. It was later that her boy friend had confronted him. The boy friend was a knife man. An old timer at any type of combat, Joe Mauser had done everything possible not to hurt him over-much. It seemed a long time ago, Joe decided. Ten years is a long time in the life of a professional mercenary. After a couple of years, you're living on borrowed time. You're living on the time of lads who went down, sacrificing some of theirs. Joe Mauser was one of the old hands who had taken much more than average borrowed time. He could remember few others who had lasted as long as he had. But now, of course, he was out of it. He was forbidden by law to participate in his former profession.

He tried to wrench his thoughts away from this sort of thing.

Max Mainz, who had started off as his batman in his last two fracases and was now his—what was he? an assistant?—said, "Holy Jumping Zen, Major, this is some hovercar. I never seen anything like it."

"They make them by hand, over in a part of Common Europe they once called Switzerland," Joe told him.

Max said admiringly, "I wouldn't think even an Upper could afford anything like this."

"An Upper-Upper gave it to me," Joe said, remembering back.

"An Upper-Upper?" Max said. "Zen! I don't think I ever even seen an Upper-Upper." He was a small man, as feisty and as ugly as a chimpanzee. For some reason Joe couldn't fathom, it seemed to endear him to women. Girls of his own caste seemed to tumble for him. Joe had never figured it out. Somehow, it isn't the Adonises in life, nor even the Herculeses, that make out

11

the most easily or the most often. Perhaps women felt a bit more secure with a little fellow like Max.

Now his companion was staring at him. He saw in Joe Mauser a man in his early thirties, about one eighty in weight, about five eleven in height and who carried himself with that calm dignity of one who had been in trouble many a time and had handled himself well. He was a moderately handsome man, and had brown hair and dark blue eyes and an even, not often smiling, mouth. His face was not particularly disfigured by the two scars, one on his chin, one on his forehead, which the cosmetic surgeons had not been completely able to erase.

Max said, in disbelief, "Gave it to you! How'd ya mean? Nobody'd give nobody something as valuable as this."

Joe chuckled sourly and said, "Max, when you've been in the fracases as long as I have and become even a minor celebrity, such as I was, you begin to attract fans, fracas-buffs who follow everything you do. They get to know more about you than you do yourself. They remember every time the situation pickled on you. They know each time you copped one and how long you were in the hospital. They clip pictures and articles from the fracas-bluff magazines such as the *Fracas Times* and paste them into albums. They get your autograph and write you fan letters."

"Sounds like a pain in the ass," Max said.

"You can't brush them off, ultimately the buffs lead to your promotion in rank, or to your being bounced up in caste level," Joe told him. "At any rate, I had a buff to end them all. She . . ."

"She?" Max protested.

"That's right. Actually, if anything, the women make more avid fracas fans than the men. This old mopsy followed my career for years, ever since I was a shavetail. She was more knowledgeable about military affairs than anyone I can remember off-hand, save possibly Field Marshal Stonewall Cogswell. I have no doubt at all but that she could have commanded a divisional magnitude fracas."

"Could have?"

"She died, well into her nineties. For years she's sent me presents. Nothing important. Watches, jewelry, clothes, things like that. But when her will was read, she'd left me this car."

Max shook his head unbelievingly. "Maybe I shoulda stayed in the fracases."

Joe said, "Max, four out of five who do either wind up very dead or with a major wound that drops them out of combat."

They turned right at Linares and drove the fifty-seven kilometers over the mountains to the ultra-highway which ran from Laredo to Mexico City. Joe opened the car up on it. After they had sped through San Luis Potosí, he began seeking out landmarks. It had been a long time since he had fought on the Guanajuato Military Reservation. More than ten years, he supposed. He had only been a staff sergeant.

The fracas had been largely a farce. It had only been of regimental magnitude and the reservation was too large to make much sense. The two forces had spent most of the time trying to seek out each other with their cavalry elements. The Category Military Department had given them a limit of one month to settle their controversy and at the end of that period Texas oil, Joe's side, was ruled to have lost, though it had been more nearly a draw.

Yes, it had largely been a farce, but it had also led to possibly the most vicious action Joe Mauser had ever fought.

They reached San Luis de la Paz and he turned right.

The road traffic immediately fell off to the vanishing point.

"This is the Guanajuato Military Reservation," Joe told Max. "The government's moved everybody out, of course. They don't use it much any more. It's good for cavalry actions but cavalry's going out in popularity. It's too hard to keep horse on the telly lenses for the sake of the drooling slobs watching the combat while they sit in their living rooms sucking on trank to keep themselves perpetually happy."

Max himself was not adverse to the institution of the fracas. He had been a buff for as long as he could remember. He said defensively, "What's wrong with being happy?"

"Nothing," Joe sighed. "But not when it's been arrived at by the use of chemicals. Real happiness is a contrast, Max. You can't have it without going through equivalent periods of sorrow. Pleasure and pain are both contrasts. You can't have either indefinitely. That's one of the reasons the concept of heaven and hell is nonsense. After a few thousand years of perpetual enjoyment, I suspect that you'd begin getting bored. And after a few thousand years in boiling oil and brimstone, I doubt if you'd any longer be in pain."

"Hey," Max protested. "You shouldn't say anything against what the Temple says and Category Religion."

"Yeah," Joe sighed. "What was good enough for Daddy is good enough for me."

"Sure," Max said in relief. He didn't want to get into an intellectual hassle with his idol.

Joe turned left just before the former town of Dolores Hidalgo.

He said, "We're coming up on San Miguel de Allende, or what's left of it. This is the town where Jim Hawkins and I nearly met our Waterloo. We damned near copped our last one."

14

"Who's Jim Hawkins?"

"Best buddy I ever had. We stuck together for the better part of a decade."

"What happened to him?" Max said, feeling an edge of jealousy. He didn't like the idea of his companion ever having a closer friend than Max Mainz.

Joe's voice went low and somewhat strained. "I had copped a minor hit in a charge in a fracas between Lockheed-Cessna and Douglas-Boeing. He didn't know it was minor and headed for the shell hole I'd fallen into. Just as he got to the rim of it, a *mitrailleuse* gun nearly cut him in two."

"Oh," Max said. "Sorry. What happened in this here town of San Miguel, whatever you called it?"

They were coming up on the former art colony now. Joe took a deep breath and said, "We were out on a scouting patrol He and I and sixteen troopers; we were trying to make contact with the enemy. We made contact all right."

They had entered the town and Joe was driving toward its center. "Up ahead there is the Zócalo," he said. "Almost all Mexican towns have one. The central park, bandstand in the middle, iron benches to relax on during the mid-day sun, fantailed grackles to sit up in the trees and shit on your head."

"Yeah, but what happened?"

"The Pemex lads happened. There were eighteen of us, armed with 30-30 carbines. There were about a hundred of them—at first. More came up later. See that church over there?"

"What church?"

"Well, it used to be a church. They shelled it down, trying to root us out. It was where they were bivouacked. When we came sneaking in, they were across the square in a former restaurant where they'd established their mess hall. All except a skeleton guard

15

they'd left in the church. We slammed into the place and finished off the guard before they knew what hit them. Most of their guns and ammunition were stacked in the church. Things had been so slow the first couple of weeks of the fracas that they'd relaxed vigilance. There were even two Vickers machine guns which we took over. They tried to storm us and we knocked them over like ten-pins. Then they settled down and tried to finish us off one by one. One of the Vickers guns was up in the bell tower. We had to keep a couple of men up there, both to operate the gun and to check out new arrivals of Pemex lads. There was practically no cover up there, so one by one we took casualties."

"Zen!" Max ejaculated. "Then what happened?"

"We sent two of the troopers out on their horses to get a message to Colonel Bomoseen, the stupid Upper who was commanding Texas Oil."

Max said, "You shouldn't oughta talk about an Upper that way, Joe. Hell, for that matter, you're a Low-Upper yourself, these days."

"Ummm," Joe said, letting the hovercar come to a halt momentarily while memories came back to him. "We'd succeeded in our mission. We found out the Pemex Lads were filtering in from this direction. He could have come up with our whole force and clobbered them. Jim and I thought we had it made. We'd get a bounce in rank, maybe even a bounce in caste. But Bomoseen was a cloddy. He didn't relieve us for three days. The others brought up mountain guns and that's why not much of the church is left. By the time it was all over, Jim and I were the only two left on our feet. He was bucking one of the Vickers guns and I had the other. Thank the Holy Jumping Zen we had all the ammunition, their ammunition, in the world. We gave them enough casualties to fill a field hospital. That's one

16

good thing about those big stone blocks that make up a church—they give good cover."

He started up again and headed up the steep street in the direction of the Queretaro road beyond. They had reached a flat stretch, just beyond a deserted hamlet. Suddenly, the hovercar stopped.

Joe Mauser scowled. This simply didn't happen. He had gotten fresh powerpacks before leaving Greater Washington. Vehicles, these days, were practically foolproof. Among other things, you had alternate, emergency motors and an alternative emergency power pack to take you to the next repair facility.

He got out and lifted the rear bonnet, and checked. He was no mechanic, but he understood the workings of a hovercar. Both of the power packs were dead—which was unbelievable.

He got back into the car, still scowling.

Max said, "What's wrong?"

"Zen if I know," Joe growled. He brought forth his pocket transceiver with the intention of calling the nearest repair facility. He didn't like to do it. It would mean that he'd have to use his credit card and that would mean a recording in the computer data banks that he had expended credit. That would mean that anyone checking, for whatever reason, would know he had been traveling through this part of the United States of the Americas.

The transceiver was dead.

Max said, "Here come a car down the road. We can hail them."

Joe Mauser had not lived in the world of the Category Military, the world of the fracases, without an instinctive something that combat men need to survive. He snapped open the dashboard compartment and snatched out his Smith & Wesson .44 and a box of cartridges.

17

"Come on," he snapped to Max. "Somebody's got an electronic damper on us."

He pushed the door open and headed for the field, calling back over his shoulder to Max, "Are you heeled?"

Max was scrambling after him. "You mean, have I gotta gun? Hell no. You're an Upper, you can carry a gun, even when you're not in a fracas. But I'm a Lower. They throw the book at you."

"Oh, wizard," Joe groaned.

Chapter Two

The country was semi-arid. Vegetation consisted of
cactus, maguey, and an occasional dwarfed mesquite
tree. The fauna, Joe knew, consisted almost exclusively
of lizards, rattlesnakes, and an occasional Gila monster.
Rabbits were few and far between. It was the kind of
country in which a sensible man preferred to be on
horseback.

Crouched low, Joe, followed by Max Mainz, plowed
as fast as he could go through the sand and gravel. He
got about one hundred feet from the car and plopped
down behind a clump of maguey, that desert plant of
Mexico from which pulque is fermented and tequila
distilled. There was a slight depression in the ground
and he flung himself into it. Max sprawled down on the
flat area beside him.

"What in the Zen's going on?" he complained
breathlessly.

"Get into the deepest depression or behind the highest ridge you can find," Joe Mauser snapped. Max was
typical of the tyro in combat. He couldn't see cover
unless it was a foot or so high.

Max obeyed orders, mystified.

"But what in hell's going on?" he said.

Joe checked the load in his long-barreled military
pistol. All six chambers were full. He opened the box of
cartridges and emptied them into the pocket of his
sport jerkin.

He said, "Somebody's out to get us, Max. They've
put an electronic damper over this vicinity and knocked
our car out and my transceiver along with it. We can't
travel and we can't communicate. I suspect that whoever it was is coming down the road in that car. You

seldom see a car on a Military Reservation, even when no fracas is in progress. There's no reason to be here. No population, no agriculture, inadequate roads. No nothing. I hope the hell they didn't spot us."

It would seem that the occupants of the other vehicle hadn't. As they approached Joe's sport hovercar they slowed considerably. Even at this distance, Joe Mauser could make out that the black sedan was full of men. It slowed, something black detached itself from it and rolled under Joe's car. Then it speeded up and took off down the road in the direction of San Miguel de Allende at a clip.

The explosion was such that it deafened Joe and Max momentarily and after a minute or two sprinklings of debris fell in their vicinity.

"A bomb!" Max blurted.

Joe grunted and took in his all but completely destroyed car. He said, "We're lucky we're not in it." Which, on the face of it, was obvious.

Down the road, the black sedan quickly turned and headed back. It came to a halt near the ruin, and five men issued forth. Even at this distance, they didn't look like locals, even if there had been any local folk. They were dressed like city people, and four of them carried pistols. But it was the fifth one that caused Joe to suck in breath. He was carrying a submachine gun. A Sten gun, by the looks of it from this distance. An old World War Two British Sten, illegal by the provisions of the Universal Disarmament Commission, backed by the New World Court which had ruled that no weapon invented since the turn of the Nineteenth Century could be manufactured, sold, used, or even possessed. Penalties for violating the Pact were stiff.

It was what had ruined Major Joseph Mauser, so far as his position in the Category Military was concerned. In a fracas in which Joe had served under Marshal

Stonewall Cogswell, Joe had flown a glider for reconnaissance. He had claimed that the glider predated the year 1900, and it did, but not the advanced type sailplane he was flying. Military observers from the Sovworld and the Neut-world hit the ceiling and brought the violation up before the International Disarmament Commission. Joe was stripped of his rank and of all his financial property, save the Inalienable Basic Common Stock which had been issued to him by the government upon his birth and which was the right of every American citizen. He was also forbidden to ever again participate in a fracas, those battles between competing corporations, a corporation and a union, or two unions fighting for jurisdiction. Even the famed Marshal Stonewall Cogswell was court-martialed, in spite of the fact that he hadn't been aware of what Joe was up to. He had been demoted to the rank of Brigadier General, a hard blow for a man of his stature and pride.

But now one of the five cautiously approached the bombed-out hovercar. He was the one carrying the submachine gun. And Joe was far from happy about it. The others, with pistols, were bad enough, outnumbering him four to one. Max was less than useless, he was a detriment, unarmed and not even used to this kind of terrain. But the Sten gun outranged Joe's revolver, in addition to its greater firepower. Joe was going to have to do something about it.

The bearer of the automatic weapon in question stepped to within about ten feet of the ruined car and cut loose with the gun, spraying the vehicle from one end to the other. They must have thought that Joe and Max were still inside and that possibly one of the other of them had survived. There was precious little chance of that, but evidently the assassins were taking no chances whatsoever.

Something came to Joe. A submachine gun was so

rare in this day and age that possibly the man who bore it was the only member of the group who knew its operation. Joe had read somewhere that there were tricky aspects to a submachine gun. You had to learn how to shoot them. The barrel would climb on you when you cut loose with a burst.

He leveled his Smith & Wesson over his left arm and took careful aim.

"Holy Zen, Joe!" Max whispered in protest. "You'll give us away."

"When they find out that we're not in that car, they're going to come looking," Joe growled back. "And our footprints aren't exactly invisible. Get ready to run for it."

His target had stopped spraying the hovercar and stood still for a moment, peering at it. Joe ever so gently squeezed the trigger and shot him squarely in the belly. The machine gunner dropped his weapon and fell like a burlap bag of feed. The others stood there, gaping at him in astonishment.

"Let's get the hell out of here," Joe rapped, immediately on his feet. He knew that the others would take a few moments to get over their surprise and another moment or so to decide on the direction from which the shot had come. Possibly Joe and Max could be out of accurate pistol range by that time. The handgun, except in the hands of an expert, isn't the most accurate weapon in the world.

He could hear Max plodding through the sand and gravel behind him. Joe had experienced country similar to this before. In fact, on this self-same Guanajuato Military Reservation. But city-bred Max Mainz was having his work cut out for him.

Joe rounded a larger than average mesquite, reached out, and grabbed the stumbling Max and drug him behind it too. Max was already panting with exertion.

Born a Low-Lower and probably used to taking trank and spending long hours sitting before the telly, rather than getting much in the way of exercise, he was in poor shape compared to Joe Mauser, in spite of his fewer years.

Joe peered around the gnarled bole of the tree.

The four were coming and Joe swore inwardly to see that one of them bore the Sten gun. He had been right; they were city dwellers and no more used to travel over this desert terrain than Max was. That was at least one advantage. But they were wise enough in the ways of combat not to bunch up. They had spread out in a row, about thirty feet between each man. There was no chance that Joe could wing a shot at one of them, miss, and have the bullet hit one of the others.

They were a bit far off and moving targets, but Joe fired two more rounds just for luck and also on the off-chance of giving them second thoughts about closing in.

But no, they kept on coming and his fire had given them indication of the location of the two fugitives. The one with the Sten gun paused momentarily and cut loose with a short burst which dug up the dirt about fifteen feet to the right of Joe and Max.

"Let's get out of here," Joe said. "We can't let that funker get close enough to get a good bead on us or we've had it."

"Right behind you," Max puffed.

They took off again and heard several pistol shots, as though at least some of their pursuers must have spotted them. But they were as ineffective as Joe's fire had been.

As he ran, he dug into his pocket and brought forth three of the .44 cartridges. He swung out the cylinder of the gun, ejected the three spent shells, and reloaded.

He looked up ahead, hoping for some indication of a

place where they could elude the gunmen, at least some area where the ground would be hard enough that it wouldn't show footprints. He doubted that the enemy was up on trailing. But no. Ahead was no sign of gullies, broken ground, or arroyos. In all directions spread the same semi-desert.

He looked back over his shoulder, past the heavily panting Max Mainz. The others were at approximately the same distance, just out of effective handgun range. He might as well conserve his ammo. The machine-gunner fired again, and again missed. Had he been a better shot he would have nailed the two fleeing men. He was probably not well acquainted with his light automatic. But it was just a matter of time before he succeeded, particularly if he closed the gap between them. Joe Mauser wondered if the killer had more than one clip for the gun. As he recalled, those World War Two submachine guns usually carried a clip of twenty rounds. If the funker had only the one clip, he'd soon have a worthless gun on his hands. He was expending bursts of four or five slugs at a time.

Joe considered going to ground and shooting it out. He suspected that he was a better, more experienced shot than any of them. But no. There was always the Sten gun to consider. And, besides, he had no way of knowing whether or not they had more bombs on hand. Even if he could find a protective hole for him and Max, one of them might crawl near enough to lob a grenade, or whatever kind of bomb they were using, into their shelter.

He looked back at Max.

The little man tried to grin, but he was obviously having a hard go of it. Sweat was pouring down his wizened face, and his shirt was sopping. He had long since shed the light jacket he had been wearing.

If it hadn't been for Max, Joe could have increased

his pace and perhaps have pulled away from the others, eventually to shake them entirely.

But he had to think of something. He couldn't let the others get near enough that his pistol could be used, due to the Sten gun. Besides, shooting it out with four men, all armed at least as well as him, didn't make sense. Joe Mauser hadn't survived fifteen years of combat by thinking of himself as a bulletproof hero.

Four to one! He had to cut those odds down some way or the other.

He slowed a bit so that Max could come up abreast of him. His own breath was coming more laboredly now, but he said, "Max, this is what we're going to have to do. We're going to have to split. You go one way, I go the other."

His companion's eyes widened. "Joe! You're not going to leave me! I don't even have no gun."

Joe said, "Two'll most likely follow me and two'll follow you. It'll give me a chance to finish off my two, then we'll get together again and see what we can do with the remaining."

"Get together again! Where? I'm lost already. Even if I got away from these funkers, I'd die of thirst out here. My tongue's already swollen up like cotton."

Joe Mauser suppressed a sigh. "No, you're not lost. We've been going very slightly up hill since we left the car. If you look back, you can see the San Miguel de Allende-Queretaro road. And you can see two spots on it that are the two cars. Now what we do is this. You head for the right, I'll head for the left. The machine-gunner is the one far to the left, so he'll undoubtedly follow me. Two of the pistol men will be after you."

"What'll I do? Where'll I meet you, Joe?"

"You'll slowly circle around, completely circle the cars, and meet me on the other side of them. I'll be able to find you. I fought in this country."

25

"If you say so," the other panted in resignation. "But I'm just about pooped, Joe. I can't keep going much longer."

Joe said, trying to keep impatience from his voice, "So are they. By the looks of them, they aren't any more familiar with this kind of country than you are. And I suspect that you're a bit younger than any of them. Damned if I know why they've kept coming after us this long. They must have one hell of a reason." He took two or three deep breaths. "Like lots of money."

"Okay, Joe," Max said. But he obviously didn't like it.

Joe said, "Keep ahead of them, just about as far as you are now. You're out of pistol range. If they slow down a bit, you can slow down too. If they stop to rest, you can stop to rest. You're not trying to completely escape from them. I doubt if you could. All you're trying to do is stay far enough ahead that they can't hit you. Somehow or other, I'll get rid of my two and then, when we get together again, we'll take on yours."

"Okay, Joe," the little man repeated.

They headed right and left.

Joe had been correct. Their pursuers divided two and two to continue the chase. In actuality, he thought, that was foolish. They should have divided three for him and one for Max. They must have discovered by now that Max had no gun. In the hour or so that had passed since first the pursuit had begun, there had been no fire from the little man. And Joe suspected that because he himself had fired only three times they believed he had only the six rounds that his gun would hold. They didn't know about his extra shells. Well, that was one small advantage. Let them think that. He'd started with twenty-six cartridges. He doubted that he'd need them all.

He could speed up now that his semi-exhausted companion was headed off in the other direction. In spite of his chosen profession, Joe Mauser had never liked combat, unlike other mercenaries, including his long-time sidekick, Jim Hawkins. But he did experience a certain exhilaration in it. A quickening of the emotions, a tensing of muscles, a sharpening of wits. And that was upon him now.

He put a little more distance between himself and the two still following, but didn't attempt to shake them entirely. He might have been able to do so and even bring himself to eventual safety. But that would leave Max to take care of himself.

Joe Mauser didn't have any plan. He couldn't figure out any way of getting to that machine-gunner without exposing himself. The area was almost flat, only a slight continuing rise. He was in open sight. There was no way he could ambush and bushwhack the others.

He continued on, slowly circling, as he had instructed Max to do, a circling that would eventually end in their meeting on the other side of the road, and on the other side of the cars. But damn little would be accomplished unless he could come up with something by that time. Something to eliminate his two men, especially the one who bore the submachine gun.

He was nearly back to the road, the others doggedly plodding along behind, the one with the Sten gun occasionally letting off a burst at him. Then he suddenly froze.

There to the right of him and not more than ten feet off was a diamondback rattlesnake. He had never seen a larger one. The deep-pitted head was drawing back into the beautiful coils and the tail, so fast moving, was not quite visible. It was making an exotic blur in the hot, still Mexican air. The skirling of the rattle was that which man, even though he has never heard it before, instantly recognizes.

Since Eden, here was man's enemy. Though the one

in Eden was reputedly soft-spoken, this one was not soft-spoken.

Old pro Joe Mauser had made a point, in his studies, usually in hospitals, or in barracks between fracases, of learning every aspect of his trade that might possibly apply to him. He had learned as much of the medic's profession as he could assimilate that applied to a man in the field. He had studied assiduously the field stripping of any weapon that he might ever use. He had studied the engineering of combat; the building of entrenchments, the sappers' know-how, the destruction of, and repair of, bridges. On vacation, between fracases, he had learned the art of climbing mountains, of swimming in rushing rivers and frozen lakes, of enduring extended hikes, without food or water. And he had studied up on running into other enemies, such as Gila monsters, large cats, wolves, bears and . . . rattlesnakes. His studies made the difference between living a year or so in the fracases and living the fifteen years that had been his.

Thus it was that Joe Mauser knew that the diamondback could only strike one third of its length, that it could only strike when in coil, and that it could only hit low. Those who customarily wore heavy high boots in rattlesnake country were going beyond need. He also knew another thing. The rattlesnake's attention span is short. If he can't strike you, very shortly he gets bored with you and forgets about it. Joe was hoping for that.

Out of immediate striking range, he froze. He looked carefully about. He spotted another snake under an outcropping of rock. And then another. And suddenly he knew where he was, what he had stumbled into. Too much of his attention had been diverted to his pursuers. He was in the middle of a desert rattlesnake den. Even as he winced at that thought, he saw still another snake, a considerably smaller one slither into a hole.

His beady-eyed confronter had gone out of coil and was not coming toward him, the rattles still proclaiming their music of war. It was getting into a position where it could go into another coil and make its try at this intruder.

Joe Mauser brought up the gun and shot it into the middle of the snake's body. It writhed, it turned over and over, it thrashed, and it showed its obscene belly, a contrast to its beautiful back. It rattled hopelessly, desperately before it died.

Joe Mauser, his lips dry, continued onward, his gun at the ready, his eyes darting. In the next few minutes he must have seen a score of snakes, but none quite as large as the one he had killed. He emerged into more of the semi-desert beyond. After fifty or sixty feet, he came to a depression, possibly half as deep as a standard combat foxhole. He took a deep breath and took his stand in it. He brought out a handful of his cartridges and stuck them head first into the sand above him, and reloaded. Then he waited, until the two gunmen came within pistol range. He fired once, and twice, and they took cover. He reloaded again.

Joe could imagine how satisfied they were with the situation. They were undoubtedly crawling forward with the utmost care. They would probably decide to come in on him from opposite sides. And when he exposed himself, the Sten gun would cut him down.

He heard the first scream in about five minutes, and the second immediately afterwards. And then the others. City hoodlums are seldom acquainted with diamondheads. Joe Mauser shuddered in compassion for them.

29

Chapter Three

He forced himself to go in fifteen minutes later. There were no snakes in sight. As he reconstructed it, they had been alarmed and enraged at the intrusion of the two crawling men into their domain and at least several must have struck. But then they had crawled into their holes.

The two were still alive, but in a complete state of shock. Joe shot them both in the head, mercifully, and took up their weapons and carefully left. He left slowly and quietly and respectful of the area through which he was traveling—and hence made it. He headed directly for the cars.

After a short distance, he stopped and sat on a boulder and examined the Sten gun. He had never held such a weapon in his hands before. He had seen the equivalent in military museums, made inoperative so as to subscribe to the Universal Disarmament Pact, firing pin removed, or whatever, but he had never held one. However, Joe Mauser was well acquainted with the world of firearms. He took his time and figured this one out.

In actuality, the Sten gun was easy to use. He had read that literally hundreds of thousands of them had been produced on a mass production basis. Many of these had been turned out with the intention of parachuting them down to the guerrillas in the Nazi rear areas, ranging from Norway to Yugoslavia and Greece. They were ultra-simple in their construction because the men who were to wield them were often peasants or factory workers without knowledge of advanced firearms.

Joe detached the clip and figured out how to extract

the round currently in the chamber. He checked the clip and then cursed himself inwardly. He should have searched the body of the man who had been carrying the weapon for additional clips. There were only eight rounds left, including the one which had been in the barrel chamber.

He wasn't going to go back into that rattlesnake den. He figured out the cocking lever, the safety, and swung the gun about, dry firing, getting the feeling, the heft of it. He wasn't going to be able to actually try it. Not with only eight rounds. However, it was not complicated. He reloaded and started back again in the direction of the cars. He knew he was in no particular hurry. Max and his pursuers, plodding more slowly over the circuitous route, wouldn't be on the scene as yet. For the first time, Joe was conscious of his thirst. The Mexican sun at that altitude of eight thousand feet was not exactly kindly.

When he got to the road, not too far from his blasted-out sports model and the black sedan of the gunmen, he spent five minutes looking up and down it, listening carefully. Then, bent double, he sped across and into the cactus and maguey beyond. He went on back to approximately the stand he and Max had taken, and settled in.

In his day, Joe Mauser had spent many an hour under cover, waiting for his quarry, many an hour in a foxhole of a trench awaiting an opportunity to fire at a foe. Every infantryman has done the same. He waited now.

Before long, Max Mainz, stumbling slowly but determinedly along, could be made out coming across the plain. And then, not too far behind, the two gunmen, also barely able to walk from weariness. They had been damn fools, Joe thought, not to have left a guard at the car. He could have stolen it and taken off, had he been willing to desert Max.

By this time, Joe Mauser had rested enough to have regained control of his breathing and steadiness of hand. He cocked the Sten gun and waited.

Max wavered across the road. Even at this distance, Joe could make out the agony in his face.

Joe Mauser leveled the gun.

The two pursuers came to the road in their turn and started across. Joe gently touched the trigger of the submachine gun and, remembering to hold the barrel down, shot a four round burst to each of them.

He came to his feet, drew his .44, and walked down to them. One was still breathing in gasps. He died as Joe came up.

Max had stopped at the sound of the machine-gun bursts, thinking the gun still in the hands of the enemy and that he was the target. Despair washed over him. He knew that he could go no farther.

But then he saw Joe Mauser, standing there over the two bodies, the Sten gun in hand. Max groaned relief and turned back.

When he had stumbled up to his companion, Joe looked at him and growled, "Damn it. I wish we could have taken one prisoner. I'd like to know who the hell they are and why they wanted to clobber us."

Max sat down on the road and put his arms around his knees and panted. He couldn't find breath to talk.

Joe went over to the field and, using the butt of the submachine gun in lieu of a shovel, dug a hole in the sand and gravel. He tossed the Sten gun into it and then filled the hole in with the side of his shoe. The more quickly he got the illegal weapon out of his hands the better. After his court-martial for violating the Universal Disarmament Pact, it would be all he needed to be caught violating it again. They'd most cheerfully throw the book at him.

There were three bodies on the road, the one he had

originally shot in the belly and the two he had just machine-gunned. One by one he took them by the heels and drug them into the desert a couple of hundred feet and hid them behind a large clump of cactus. He searched the bodies but came up with no indication of identity, not even universal credit cards.

Scuffing out the marks of the dragging with the side of his shoe, he went back to Max and said, "Come on. Let's get out of here. It's probably unlikely, but there just might be more of them in the vicinity."

He helped the smaller man to his feet and they headed for the abandoned black sedan the killers had arrived in. It was an old-fashioned, wheeled vehicle, a gasoline burner. That made sense. They couldn't have entered the area they had blanketed with their electronic damper in a hovercar. A gasoline vehicle was operative where a power pack car wasn't. Happily, the hoodlums had left the keys in it.

They got into the front seat and Joe took over the driver's position. He handed Max the pistol he had confiscated from the fallen killer in the rattlesnake den.

Max had finally caught his breath. "It's against the law for a Military Reservation," he said.

Even as he started up, Joe had to laugh. He said, "It's also against the law for somebody to kill you, but those five tried to do it. As long as people are shooting at you, Max, shoot back if you can, and the hell with the law. You can work out your problems with the law later—if you're still alive." .

Max tucked the gun into a side pocket and said, "How in the name of Holy Jumping Zen did you manage to kill those other two and get that machine gun, Joe?"

"I didn't. At least not directly. They made the mistake of crawling through a den of diamondhead rattlesnakes."

The little man shivered. He said, "I never seen a snake, but I'm afraid of them."

Tensions evaporating, Joe Mauser laughed. They were underway now, headed once more for Queretaro. Joe was hoping that they had enough gas to make it to Mexico City, which was about one hundred and fifty miles to the south.

Max, recovering rapidly, said, "How in the name of Zen did they know where to find us?"

Joe thought about it. "Somebody planted a directional bug in the car, somewhere tucked away, so that they could zero in on it. It had to be done back in Greater Washington, possibly while it was parked in our apartment building garage. So most likely whoever engineered the attempt to crisp us is Washington-based. Those five men, by the way, weren't Mexicans. They were of Northern European extraction."

Max wasn't up on this sort of thing. He said, "Couldn't they have been Mexican?"

Joe shook his head. "It's unlikely."

To Joe's relief, they ran into no more trouble on the Guanajuato Military Reservation. Once on the ultrahighway again, with its heavy traffic, it seemed unlikely that any attempt would be made on them. At Queretaro he turned left and made time in the direction of Mexico City. The gasoline held out, which was another relief. Now, more than ever, he wanted to refrain from using his universal credit card. His sports hovercar had been well bombed, but sooner or later the authorities were going to find it. His only chance was to get back to Greater Washington and put in a report that it had been stolen. He doubted that they would find the boides. He doubted that they would even look for them. Even if they did, they'd have their work cut out for them puzzling through what had happened. Three bodies were hidden, and two were up in the rattlesnake den. Presumably, the whole five could have been in on the theft of Joe's hovercar. Then, for whatever reason, they had fallen out. The two killed the other three, hid their bodies, and took off into the desert after blowing up the car. They had wound up in the rattlesnake den and were killed there. In a day or two the buzzards would have stripped them, and there would be no evidence remaining that Joe had finished them off with his pistol. At least, that's what he hoped they would think. Thank the powers that be that Frank Hodgson was the actual working head of the North American Bureau of Investigation. He could suppress just about anything.

Joe Mauser had been in Mexico City before. He drove around the ultra-highway that circled it until he arrived at Reforma, and then drove in toward the center. In its day, Mexico City had been one of the most beautiful capitals in the world. This was no longer its day. Like most of the world's cities with a multi-million population, it had deteriorated. Who would wish to live in a major city if it wasn't necessary? And in these days of People's Capitalism and the Ultra-Welfare State, it wasn't necessary for about ninety percent of the population. Given your Inalienable Basic Common Stock, issued to every citizen at birth, and reverting to the government upon death, you could live anywhere you wished, particularly if you weren't one of the few lucky enough to secure employment and thus be able to augment your income. You could live on the beaches, in the mountains, in the forests, in a climate of your choice. If you subsisted on the dividends from only your Inalienable Basic you weren't rich, but at least you didn't have to live in a city slum.

Joe drove through Chapultepec Park, and emerged onto Paseo de la Reforma, one of the most beautiful boulevards in the world. He checked the address which

Miss Mikhail, of Philip Holland's office, had given him, and at Dinamarca he turned right. He parked the car at the corner near the Avenue Chapultepec.

He said to Max, who had been staring out the window in fascination, "Wizard. We'll dump this wagon here and go on by foot. I'd think it would take them a couple of days, at least, to locate it and check it out. By that time, Zen willing, we'll be back in Greater Washington. I hope this guy Zavala has the funds to advance us for a couple of tickets."

The address of Jesus Zavala was at the corner of Chapultepec and Morelia. It turned out to be an impressive looking office building. They entered the lobby and looked up at the directory. Jesus Zavala was a dentist. They took the elevator to the fifth floor and located the office. By the looks of it, Zavala wasn't going to have much difficulty shelling out for two tickets on the airline for them. There was no one in the reception room save a pretty Mexican girl behind the desk.

Joe said to her in Spanish, "Is the doctor in?"

She smiled at him and answered in Amer-English. He was obviously not a Mexican. She said, "Do you have an appointment Señor?"

"I'm afraid not, Señorita. This isn't a business call."

"Your name, please?"

"Joseph Mauser."

Her eyes widened. "*Major* Joe Mauser?"

Damn. Just his luck to run into a fracas fan. He had hoped that no one would recognize him here in Mexico City. She'd probably tell all her fracas-buff friends that she'd met the famous Joe Mauser. He hoped that he wouldn't get into the local news.

"Not major, any more," he told her. "I've been disqualified to participate in the fracases."

"You'll always be Major Joe Mauser to me, sir. I've

watched you on telly a dozen times. Everybody I know thinks you got a very raw deal because of that glider thing."

"Thanks," Joe said. "The doctor?"

"Yes, sir. Of course." She did the things receptionists do, then looked up and said, "Go right in, Major."

Joe Mauser went through the door next to her desk, trailed by Max who slipped her a wink as he passed.

Jesus Zavala looked up from his desk. He was a man in his fifties, darker of complexion than even most Mexicans. His sparkling white teeth were a good advertisement for his trade. He wore a Van Dyke beard which was beginning to show traces of grey and old-fashioned glasses, in this day of contact lenses or eye surgery. He was almost as small as Max and thinner. His clothes were conservative and some twenty years out of date.

Joe looked at him and said, "Progress."

The others eyebrows went up. "Indeed," he said. And then, "It must be resumed."

Chapter Four

Joe nodded at the response to the password and said, "I've been sent from national headquarters."

"Indeed. For what purpose?" The dentist had come to his feet. He shook hands across the desk with first Joe, and then Max.

Joe looked around the room. "Is there any possibility at all that this room is bugged?"

"Bugged?"

Joe said, "An electronic microphone to pick up any conversations that take place. They've got some fantastically advanced models these days."

The other looked startled. "It never occurred to me."

Max said, "I'd hate to be the cloddy who had to monitor a dentists office. The screams would give me ulcers before the week was out."

Zavala looked at him questioningly, then back to Joe. He said, "The girl gave me your name, of course, Señor Mauser. And I am familiar with it. I followed the news of your remarkable duel with the Hungarian in Budapest. However... this gentleman?"

"Names aren't important," Joe said, avoiding introducing Max. "Is there someplace we can talk that we absolutely *know* couldn't be bugged?"

The dentist looked at his wrist chronometer and said, "Have you eaten?"

"Only sandwiches and such for the past three days," Joe told him.

"Then, let us go. It's my lunch hour and I have no appointments until four."

Joe said, "I see that the institution of the siesta is still with us in Mexico."

They filed out, Max tipping the girl another wink as

he went by. She smiled at him. Joe had a sneaking suspicion that given a few days in town Max would have her in the sack in short order. Especially if he told her he was Category Military and had fought in the fracases.

The small, thin dentist led the way to the street and then to the nearest entry to the famous Mexico City Metro. Some stations had small Aztec pyramids or temples in them, which were found when the underground was being excavated.

Max said, "Subway? Don't you have no vacuum-tube transport in this here town?"

The dentist looked at him testily. "To some extent, but we also have the metro for mass transportation. What I had in mind was the fact that anyone attempting to trail us through the mobs that press into metro cars would have quite a problem on their hands."

"Good thinking," Joe said. "Let's all keep our eyes peeled for anyone who looks as though he's tailing us."

They got out at the station at the far end of Alameda Park near the Bellas Artes building, turned right down San Juan de Letran, and then left at the next street.

"Here we are," Zavala said. "*Prendes*. One of the oldest restaurants in Mexico City. Emiliano Zapata once rode in here on his horse, gun in hand, seeking an enemy."

"How's the food?" Max said cynically.

The dentist didn't answer.

The *Prendes* certainly looked like one of the oldest restaurants in Mexico City. In fact, it looked like one of the oldest restaurants anywhere.

"Many of we Mexicans like the old ways," Zavala said to Joe, no apology in his voice.

"Can't blame you," Joe said. "Looks like a damn good place to get a meal."

The dentist, being acquainted with the specialties,

made suggestions and ordered for them. Largely, it was seafood, though the steak Max selected was probably the first real steak he had ever eaten in his life. Mexicans, Zavala explained, didn't go for commercial whale meat from the herds now being exploited by the whale "cowboys" with their porpoise assistants. The food was accompanied by the darkest, richest, and strongest beer Joe Mauser had ever tasted.

Joe looked around at the hundreds of persons, ninety-five percent male, packed into the place, and then back to Jesus Zavala. He said. "Do you mean this is the quiet place where we can talk?"

The other smiled. "My dear Señor Mauser, have you ever been anywhere more conducive to secret conversation than a popular businessman's restaurant at lunch time? In this babble, no one will hear us, or bother to try. Over this babble, our voices could not be heard at the next table."

Joe grunted in acceptance. "I guess you're right."

As they waited for their dishes, Zavala said, "Now, then, the purpose of your visit. You say that you come from national headquarters."

Joe Mauser nodded. "Evidently, you were contacted by one of our rank-and-file members here in Mexico City. He reported that you were one of the leaders of a loosely-organized local group which had independently come to much the same conclusions that our larger organization has."

Zavala looked at him. "That seems true. Have you ever drunk tequila?"

"Yes," Joe said, repressing an inner wince.

"No," Max said.

The dentist snapped his fingers at a scurrying waiter, who hurried over.

Their host ordered in Spanish, then said to his guests, "The tequila they have here is unlike anything that I know of in Mexico."

40

The waiter came scurrying back with a bottle of golden colored liqueur. From old and hard experience, so far as Joe Mauser was concerned, tequila was as white as vodka or gin. A plate of quartered limes and a shaker of salt came with it.

Joe didn't want to lose points with his host. He said to Max, "Now this is how you do it. You pour yourself a sizeable slug of the tequila. Then you take up the salt and sprinkle a bit of it on the back of your hand. You lick the salt and then take up your tequila and knock it back in one quick, stiff-wristed motion. Then, real quick, you pick up a quarter of the lime and bite into it—before you die."

Jesus Zavala laughed appreciatively. "With this tequila, you won't die."

They went through the performance, and didn't die. Zavala had been correct. This tequila must have been laid down in the stone age. Joe, in his experiences on the Mexican military reservations, had never tasted anything so smooth. It reminded him of French cognac.

"Hey," Max said. "You could build up a taste for this here guzzle." He poured himself another.

The dentist cleared his throat before saying, "Ah, the aging has made it smooth, but it is nevertheless potent."

"Yeah," Max said happily. "And that's what I need. Something potent. This morning me and Joe was out in the desert with five men shooting at us."

Jesus Zavala stiffened somewhat and looked at Joe.

Joe Mauser said, "Evidently, the party is getting a little rough. Surely you didn't expect it not to get rough. You don't play at revolution."

"When my friends and I began to get together and discuss alternatives to People's Capitalism we weren't thinking in terms of violence," Zavala said.

"We aren't either," Joe told him, "if we can avoid it. But possibly we can't. Somebody was pointing out to me just the other day that individuals among a ruling

41

class, clique or caste, might be converted to a basic change. An extreme example is the fact that Karl Marx and Frederick Engels were both upper class: Engels, in particular, was a wealthy manufacturer. But the ruling class as a whole invariably refuses to step down to make way for a new socioeconomic system. A socioeconomic system like a living organism does not want to die and will do anything in its power to continue to live."

"Then your organization does advocate force and violence to overthrow People's Capitalism, the Ultra-Welfare State?" Zavala said, somewhat coldly.

Their food had arrived then and they held their peace until the waiter had served them and departed.

When he was gone, Joe said, "Force, but not necessarily violence."

Jesus Zavala looked at him questioningly.

Joe tasted the dish the dentist had recommended. It was the whitefish that grow only in Mexico's Lake Patzcuaro. He decided it was the most delicate fish he had ever sampled.

He said, "You can have force without violence. For instance, when a majority of the people vote for something they are exerting a force. Suppose you combine the two. You organize everybody in the country you can who still works and votes. You would have a lot of force to bring to bear, but you wouldn't be advocating violence and consequently present laws couldn't get to you."

The dentist pursed his lips. "But suppose the other side, the ruling class which doesn't want to step down, in short, the Uppers, resorted to violence?"

Joe nodded. "Forming such organizations as the Nathan Hale Society. Then we'd have to take whatever steps seemed necessary. But keep in mind that the Uppers number less than one percent of the population. And even some of them will undoubtedly come over to

42

us. In fact, some already have." He took another bite of the delicious fish. "I'm a Low-Upper, for instance."

Zavala was surprised. "You are?" He scowled, then added, "I'm an Upper Middle."

Joe nodded again. "Actually, I was born a Lower and slowly worked my way up in the Category Military to Mid-Middle. After my court-martial I was chosen to go on a semi-espionage assignment to the Sov-world. To give me prestige in the eyes of the Sovs, who are even more status-symbol conscious than our Upper caste, I was bounced to Low-Upper."

Max said happily, "This is the best meat I ever laid a lip over." He took another pull at his beer.

The Mexican said to Joe, "How would you sum up your goals?"

"It's all in our passwords," Joe answered. "Progress, it must be resumed. Our society is in a rut. The Uppers don't want change. You start allowing changes and they'll get out of hand. They don't want to rock the boat, upset the applecart. So any changes at all are frowned upon. Projects such as the space program have been discontinued, along with practically all scientific research. However, automation and computerization have enabled us to solve the problems of production with a minimum of labor. In fact, nine out of ten of the population, largely Lowers, are unemployed and live on the Ultra-Welfare State. That's got to end. A society that utilizes only one tenth of its labor power is obviously static and slated for the dust heap. Rome is a good example. The Roman proletariat was given free food and free circuses to keep them amused. They were in complete idleness while slaves did the work."

"And we have much the same situation today," Zavala mused. "We give our people shares of Inalienable Basic Common Stock, which they cannot sell, even if they wish to. All their lives they collect their dividends from it. Then we give them the drug trank, non-additive, non-physically harmful, to keep them in a continual happy daze. And on top of that we give them all the violence they want on telly."

"That's right," Joe said. "Unfortunately, among those tens of millions of largely uneducated Lowers are undoubtedly potential geniuses in science, the arts, and technology."

The other took off his glasses, brought forth a handkerchief, and polished them. He kept his eyes on Joe, questioningly. "And how are you coming, thus far in your program?"

Joe Mauser shrugged. "At this point, the mass organization hasn't begun to form as yet. What we're doing is gathering cadres, getting together basic groups who will one day become teachers. That's why I've been sent down here. Thus far, we've only got a few members in this city. If you have a group that will come over to us, then we've taken a good step in Mexico City."

The other nodded and took the last bite of the Pacific crayfish he had ordered. He said, "To go back a little. You pointed out that ninety percent of our people have been displaced by the automation and computerization of our industries. You pointed out that a progressive society must utilize its manpower. Very well, what work can you give them?"

"There's other work besides industry," Joe told him. "We no longer have to do much in the way of the old drudgery. But there are the arts, the sciences, advanced technology. Once again, things like space. We're stagnating. We've got to get back under way again. There are still diseases that we haven't licked as yet. We still have one helluva way to go to really beautify this continent. Given this new society we're working for, the education program alone would be staggering. Under People's Capitalism, the Lowers and even to a certain extent the Low-Middles and Mid-Middles have deli-

44

berately been uneducated. An educated man is a dangerous man. Of the lower castes, only the Upper-Middles have the opportunity to get a really adequate education. After all, somebody has to run the country, and most of the Uppers are too damn lazy or stupid to do it."

Max sighed in satisfaction and put down his knife and fork. "What've you two been talking about?" he said.

Joe looked at him and shook his head in despair. "Women," he said. "Mopsies."

They had finished eating. The restaurant's customers were beginning to thin out. Their host motioned to a waiter and requested cigars. Another waiter cleared the table.

Max said expansively, "I'm an authority. You shoulda consulted me."

Zavala looked over at him and said, "You mentioned being shot at by five men in the desert. What happened?"

"Damned if I know," Max said plaintively. "It happened too confusing for me to ever figure it all out. Joe, here, finished them off."

The Mexican looked at Joe Mauser in awe. He said, "All of them? Five?"

Joe said, "It was pure luck. Rattlesnakes took some of them. By the way, they didn't look like Mexicans. The best way I can figure it, they were sent from Greater Washington to finish me—and Max, of course. Which would indicate an organization opposed to ours. And, to be frank, that indicates in turn that there is danger in belonging to our outfit. You should consider . . ."

"We Mexicans are not cowards, Señor Mauser," Zavala said stiffly. "The fact that gunmen might be sent against us will not alter our decision whether or not to join you."

"Of course not," Joe said hurriedly. "By the way,

how many are there in your organization?"

"We started as an informal discussion group of about ten of my friends and colleagues."

"Only ten?" Joe said in disappointment.

"But our number has now swollen to over two hundred."

"Two hundred!"

"Yes. All are of Middle caste, except one. Since we are a democratic organization, it will be necessary that you meet and address them, and that we put to a vote whether or not to amalgamate with you."

"Meet two hundred? I'm in a hurry to get back to Greater Washington to report that my hovercar is missing. It was destroyed in the fight. I want it to seem that it was stolen. It is impractical for it to come out that I've been in Mexico City."

"It's no problem," the dentist told him, scratching his little beard. "I mentioned that all of us are Middles save one. He is a Mid-Upper and owns an extensive hacienda. The banquet hall is sufficient in size to contain us all. You can address us, and then we will take our vote."

"Wizard," Joe said. "Now, here's a problem. I want to refrain from using my, or Max's, universal credit card. But we must have quarters tonight and somebody to buy us airline tickets for Greater Washington tomorrow. Under assumed names, obviously."

"That, my friend, is no problem," the dentist said. "One of us is a travel agent and can handle all the red tape." He came to his feet. "Shall we return to my office? I will take the steps to call the meeting for tonight and will then drive you to our Mid-Upper's mansion. Without doubt, he will gladly put you up tonight, after the meeting."

He put his credit card in the table's payment slot, while Joe and Max also tossed their napkins to the table and stood.

46

Max took one last look at the Pancho Villa mural as they left. He said, admiringly, "They musta really had fracases in them days."

Chapter Five

The meeting in the hacienda of the Mexican Mid-Upper had been a roaring success. Joe had talked for about two hours, in all, and then had a question period that extended well into the night. The fact was that they had already come to most of the conclusions that Joe's organization had. He had only to clear them up on a few points.

Jesus Zavala, obviously well respected in the group, had explained it to Joe after the others had left, save for their host, of course.

He had said, "When a basic politico-economic change is needed, it isn't just one group that comes along and advocates the change. A dozen, a score, of individuals and groups of varying sizes suddenly materialize, each independently of the others. If there is a truth, it will come to more than one, or more than a few. There will be student groups, possibly women's groups, all spontaneously heading in the same direction. As things come to a head, obviously they will unite and achieve victory together. That is what happened here in Mexico City. We had never even heard of your organization based in Greater Washington, but we arrived at the same conclusions you had a bit earlier. The only thing that makes sense is for our two groups to amalgamate."

Yes, the meeting was a roaring success and the Mexicans had voted unanimously to align themselves with Hodgson's and Holland's underground movement. Joe hadn't revealed the names of the two ultimate leaders; contact would be made by lower-echelon members, such as Joe Mauser. The fewer who knew the identity of the two men who had worked their way up

48

to the highest levels of the government of the United States of the Americas, the better.

He and Max spent the night at the hacienda, and in the morning they took the two airline tickets that were secured for them, in assumed names, and were driven to the airport. After high sounding tributes from their host and Jesus Zavala, they took their places in the shuttle rocket to Greater Washington.

"Zen!" Max said. "I never been on one of these before. All I been in is jets and not too very often."

"They're faster," Joe said laconically. "You get there in a few minutes. In fact, you get there before your heart comes down from out of your throat."

At the shuttle-port in Greater Washington they took a double-seater vacuum-tube transport capsule and emerged in the closet-like terminal in their own apartment.

Joe and Max were living together in a two-bedroom apartment superior to anything either of them had ever called home before. Joe had only recently been raised to the rarified altitudes of being a Low-Upper and had hence had his Inalienable Basic stock augumented considerably. And even Max's had been increased somewhat upon his reaching Mid-Lower status. But on top of this, Hodgson and Holland had seen that they acquired additional shares of Variable Basic, supposedly as a result of their trip to Budapest. What they had really done there, the higher ups would never know. Phil Holland had cooked up an entirely fictitious report.

At any rate, they split the costs of the apartment, two-thirds from Joe, who had it to splurge, and one-third from Max. In actuality, they had never figured out why. Max had started as Joe's batman in the Vacuum Tube Transport versus Continental Hovercraft affair, and then continued on with him after that fracas was over. But now that Joe Mauser was no longer in the Category Military, Max remained on. In a way he performed like a servant, but in other ways he seemed more a companion, an assistant, a friend. Neither of them attempted to define their relationship.

Joe went into the living room and to the auto-bar and dialed himself a Cooler.

He said to Max, over his shoulder, "Drink?"

"Sure. You think they got any of that there tequila, up here?"

"I would imagine so. Straight, or a Margarita?"

"What's a Margarita?"

"Mixed drink. Tequila, Cointreau, lime juice, salt on the rim of the glass. Makes a good cocktail."

"I'll take it straight, like we had in the restaurant in Mexico City yesterday."

Joe dialed for him and when the drinks had arrived, he went over to a comfort chair and sat down, after bringing his transceiver from his pocket. He dialed Doctor Nadine Haer, his fiancée.

Her face lit up on the small screen of the portable tellyphone and she said, "Darling! I thought that you were out of town."

"I was," he told her. "We just got back. I've got quite a report to make."

She said, "FH is up in New York but PH is due at my house this evening. You could meet him there."

"Good. I don't like to go to either of their offices too often. Might begin to raise comment."

She said, "Look darling. You caught me driving along in a hovercab. I'm quite near your place. Why don't you go downstairs to the curb and wait for me and we'll go to lunch together at the Swank Room? We'll work up an appetite walking over. It's a lovely day."

"My arm has been twisted. I'm always forgetting that now that I'm an Upper, I'm eligible to enter the Swank Room. However, I'm a little on the grimy side. Wait for me in the lobby. I'll take a quick shower and get a change of clothes and be right down."

"Wizard. See you, darling." Her face faded.

Max was scowling into his glass. He grumbled, "This isn't as good as the stuff the doc bought us in Mexico City."

Joe Mauser went into his bedroom and cleaned up in record time.

Back in the living room he said to Max, "I'm going to lunch with Nadine. Why don't you take the balance of the day off?"

"Sure, Boss."

In the lobby, Joe came up on Nadine Haer while she was watching a broadcast of the news. It came to him, all over again, how unbelievably pretty she was. In the past, he had thought that her features were more delicate than those to whom he was usually attracted and that her lips were less full. But he had changed that opinion after falling in love with her. She was dressed beautifully, which was understandable in view of the fact that she held a sizeable chunk of the stock of Vacuum Tube Transport, currently one of the hottest transport corporations in the country. Not to speak of her dividends from Inalienable Basic issued to a Mid-Upper.

He grinned at her and said, "Watching a fracas?"

She came quickly to her feet and smiled. "That'll be the day. I just picked up a news flash from Mexico. They've found a bombed-out sports hovercar and, noticing a lot of vultures in the vicinity, found in turn five dead men, at least some of whom had been shot. Wasn't your assignment in Mexico, Joe?"

"Oh, oh," he said. "Already? Just a moment, Nadine." He brought forth his transceiver and dialed the police. When a sergeant's face faded in, Joe said crisply, "I'm Joseph Mauser. Formerly Category

51

Military, Rank Major. Low-Upper." He gave his identity number. "I wish to report a stolen sports hovercar."

"Yes, sir," the sergeant said respectfully. "Do you remember the license plate number, sir?"

Joe Mauser gave it to him.

The sergeant said, "Yes, sir. We'll get in touch with you as soon as we get a report on it, sir. It shouldn't be too difficult. The traffic computers will get a cross on your car. How long's it been gone?"

"I don't know," Joe said. "I haven't used it for several days. It was parked in the garage of my apartment house. It might have disappeared three or four days ago, or possibly as late as this morning. It just came to my attention a few minutes ago " He gave the officer the address of his building, though the other could have easily checked that on Joe's dossier.

"Thank you, sir," the other said and his face faded.

Joe put his transceiver back into his pocket and turned to face Nadine again. She had her lower lip in her teeth and was looking at him questioningly.

She said, as a doctor ever in rebellion against violence, "Joe! You didn't kill those five men, did you? Five?"

"It was their lives or those of Max and me."

"Oh, Joe, why are these things always happening to you?"

He looked at her in exasperated despair. "I obviously don't want them to," he told her, keeping irritation from his voice. "Let's go, dear."

She had been right. It was a lovely day for a stroll in Greater Washington. They both felt exhilarated in each other's company. It was a new romance, but already they were engaged.

As they were passing through a park and passing an iron bench, a voice said, "Hi, Captain."

52

Joe frowned momentarily, but then came to a halt and said, "Why, it's Ferd Dalton. Sergeant Ferd Dalton."

The man grinned. "As ever was."

The other had mechanical limbs where his right arm and right leg had once been, but he was obviously a double-amputee. The lines in his otherwise fairly youthful face indicated that he had been through a great deal of pain.

Joe turned to Nadine and said, "Darling, this is Sergeant Ferd Dalton, an old comrade in arms. Ferd, this is my fiancée, Doctor Nadine Haer."

Dalton grinned again and said, "You don't look like a doctor."

And Nadine smiled back and said, "What does a doctor look like?"

Joe said to him, "Let's see, your wife's name was Molly, wasn't it?"

"Yeah, Molly." The other's face went rueful. "Well, we kind of drifted apart after I copped this last one. Mortar shell."

Joe inwardly winched. Ferd and Molly Dalton had been more than usually close. He suspected that when Ferd had taken the mortar hit, more than his arm and leg had been affected. He suspected that the other could no longer perform as a man.

Joe said, "Otherwise, how's it been going, Ferd?"

The sergeant shrugged it off. "Oh, so, so. The only income I've got is my Inalienable Basic. Once I was discharged from the hospital I was on my own. From time to time extra medical bills come up and I've got to meet them. Those Category Military bastards, don't give a damn about a disabled veteran."

Joe said, "We've got to hurry along, Ferd. But, listen, give me your I.D. number and one of these days I'll phone you on your transceiver and we'll get together."

"Sure, Captain," the former sergeant said and rattled it off.

Joe copied it down and he and Nadine said their goodbyes and walked on, Joe looking thoughtful.

When they were out of sight of Ferd Dalton, Joe brought his transceiver from his pocket and dialed the Banking Data Banks. He gave the pertinent information and then said, "I wish to transfer one share of Variable Basic Common stock from my account to this one." He read off Ferd Dalton's I.D. number.

The phone screen said, "Transaction completed."

Nadine looked at him from the side of her eyes. "Zen!" she said. "If you did that with every man you were in combat with, you'd be stripped."

"Yeah," Joe said, his voice empty. "If I donated a share of Variable to every lad who saved my life in my time, I'd be stripped. Trouble is, I don't know how to locate most of them—those who are still alive."

"And Ferd Dalton saved your life?"

"We were in the swamps, in the Louisiana Military Reservation. Pinned down by a Maxim gun. I'd taken two hits. I was a captain then. The rest of my lads managed to sneak off but Ferd stuck with me. We were about half in and half out of swamp water and that queer grass they have down there. The second day, I became delirious and he had to keep my head up out of the water. We were three days in the swamp."

Her face was pale. "Don't tell me any more about it, Joe."

He said, "It has a happy ending. Here I am."

In spite of the fact that she had just asked to drop the subject, she couldn't help saying, "How often did you get into spots like that?"

"I can't remember," he said quite truthfully "Ah, here's the Swank Room."

The Swank Room was quite the swankest restaurant

in Greater Washington and for the Upper caste alone, of course. Joe Mauser had been in it exactly once before, as a guest of Nadine Haer. Even then, the management might have frowned had it not been for the fact that Joe Mauser at the time was a fracas celebrity. It boasted not only live waiters in livery, but a small orchestra.

As they followed the waiter captain to their table, they passed fairly near the bandstand. The orchestra leader winked at Joe and the dance tune they were playing was dropped. The orchestra swung into the lilting "The Girl I Left Behind Me."

> ...I knew her heart was breaking,
> And to my heart in anguish pressed
> The girl I left behind me.

It was the old Civil War marching song. Custer's Seventh Cavalry had rode out to it on their way to their rendezvous with Sitting Bull's Sioux at the Little Big Horn.

Joe chuckled inwardly. It was part of the fling that telly cameraman Freddy Soligen had sold him on some time ago. Freddy, as ambitious to accumulate bounces in caste as was Joe, was of the opinion that heroes were made, not born. The fracas buffs wanted glamorous heroes; they didn't have the ability to recognize a good soldier when they saw one, a man capable of conducting a retreat or officering a holding action. They wanted gore and they wanted glamor. Freddy had pointed out that such big names as Colonel Ted Sohl and Captain Jerry Sturgeon had never copped one in their lives. The dashing Ted Sohl had two western type pistols belted to his waist, and a romantic limp and a craggy face. A specially built pair of boots gave him the limp, Freddy told Joe. So Freddy Soligen had designed a special uniform resembling that of an Austrian hussar, and provided Joe with a theme song, "The Girl I Left Behind Me." He then bribed orchestra leaders to play it every time Joe entered a nightclub or restaurant. He also bribed fracas buff magazines to run laudatory articles about Joe, and telly show reporters to interview him. All this paid for by Joe Mauser, of course, from his life savings. The theory was that he would eventually be bounced up to Upper caste and then he, in turn, would help Freddy Soligen. It had all gone well, until he had pulled his spectacular, which was to make him the hero of them all. The glider thing had fizzled, and he'd wound up with his court-martial.

Seated, they ordered their meals, and when the waiter was gone, Joe looked around at their expensively-garbed neighbors and said, with a shake of the head, "You know, I still can't get used to associating with Uppers."

Nadine said, "They're no different than anyone else. As a matter of fact, they probably average in intelligence and ability less than the Middles. An hereditary aristocracy invariably deteriorates. They have no motivation. Why bother to take your studies seriously when play is more fun? Why bother to work at a serious job, when you don't need money?"

"Well, that doesn't apply to all of them," Joe said, just to be saying something.

"Damn near all," she muttered. "Those that do anything at all take jobs such as political ones, or as heads of corporations, or as diplomats, or bishops of the Temple in Category Religion. Or, when they join the Category Military, they immediately become at least colonels and precious seldom do they get—what do you call it?—into the dill. They hold down positions far behind the lines."

Joe had to laugh. It was all too true, especially the Category Military bit. It was uncanny the way Upper officers managed to stay out of the line of fire when the situation had pickled.

He said, "I wonder how it all got started, this dividing our people into nine castes, ranging from Upper-Upper down to Low-Lower. We started off with a free and equal people."

"Joe, Joe, you innocent," Nadine said. "We used to pride ourselves on the lack of classes in the history of the United States, but we've been among the most class-ridden societies of modern times, right from the beginning. I assume that you don't labor under the illusion that the men who froze and starved under Washington at Valley Forge were later allowed to vote for or against him when he ran for President. Only the equivalent of Uppers in that day were allowed to vote. Only one out of five adults in the United States were eligibile to vote in Washington's election."

"Oh, come on now," Joe said in protest.

"All right, let's start from the beginning. First of all, all women were eliminated. Betsy Ross might have been great sewing the first flag. Molly Pitcher might have fought side by side with her husband at the battle of Monmouth and might, as the heroic story goes, have taken over his gun when he fell. And Dolly Madison might have been the most charming hostess and the most witty woman ever to grace the White House. Or do you know the story of Margaret Corbin? Upon the death of her husband at the attack on Fort Washington in 1776, she commanded his cannon until she was seriously wounded; she later became the first woman in American history to be pensioned by the government. In 1916 her remains were moved to West Point, where a monument was erected in her honor. But neither she nor any of the others I named were ever allowed to vote."

"The last of the women-libbers," Joe smiled at her.

Two waiters came up with their food, and they held their peace until served.

When the waiters were gone, Joe said, "Admittedly,

women didn't get the vote until after the first World War, but that doesn't add up to only one out of five adults being able to vote."

She went on, slightly flushed in the heat of argument. On her, Joe decided, it looked fine.

"Very well," she said. "Then there were the Negroes of the time. Slaves. Obviously they didn't have the vote. But besides women and Blacks, there were men who didn't have property qualifications, such as workers in the cities, merchant seamen, privates and non-coms in the military, and farmers whose farms were too small. Property requirements existed in all thirteen of the United Colonies. In short, the poor didn't vote. Nor, in some, if not all, of the States, did those who were under-educated. Educational requirements prevailed in many of the States until well into the 20th Century. Oh, we had our equivalent of Lowers from the very beginnings of the Republic."

She took a decisive bite of her food.

"I surrender," Joe said. "But what I was really wondering about was the origin of our present castes. You'll admit we didn't have them in the old days."

"It took place over a period of time," she said, after taking another bite. "According to one of the old polls, back in the mid-20th century, eighty-five percent of the American people thought of themselves as Middle-Class, even many of those perpetually on relief. However, with the coming of wholesale relief and the point where more than half of the population was on relief, the term Lower Class came in. Those who still worked began to be called Middle Class, no matter what kind of work they did. And the wealthy began being called Upper Class. In time, as People's Capitalism came in, you became more or less frozen into the class in which you were born. It was diffucult to bounce yourself up, particularly when the lower classes couldn't afford higher education and education had become a must to get a job in modern industry, or one of the professions. Finally, each class was split into three levels. The Upper-Middles were largely doctors, university level professors, scientists and so forth. The Middle-Middles were largely technicians, engineers, teachers in lower education. The Low-Middles were largely skilled workers and junior technicians. The Upper-Lowers were the unemployables and soon became the majority of the population, the scum of society."

Joe said, "Why do we always get into these squabbles, which usually wind up with you giving me a lecture? Let's talk about something more interesting."

"Such as what," she said severely. "Your socioeconomic education has been sorely neglected, and we both belong to an organization dedicated to overthrowing the present politico-economic system."

"Such as us. When are we going to be married? I can't wait much longer."

She put her fork down and looked at him compassionately. She said, her voice low, "I'm afraid it's going to have to be put off indefinitely, darling."

"What!"

"The details are beyond me. The lawyers have tried to explain, but I know nothing about law. However, if I marry, evidently there are some loopholes that would allow my brother, Balt, to take over the greater part of my holdings in Vacuum Tube Transport. You see, with the death of my father, Balt became the new Baron Haer, although he himself has little of the stock. For inheritance reasons, tax reasons, father had transferred most of his own holdings to Balt. When it seemed obvious that Continental Hovercraft would win the fracas between the two corporations, Balt secretly sold all the stock and invested it in Continental. But through your efforts, we didn't lose. Balt, infuriated at you, sold his Continental at a great loss and reinvested in our corporation. But he doesn't have much voting power now."

Joe said, "What in the hell's all this got to do with our marriage?"

"I tell you, Joe darling, I don't know all of the details. But Balt is now the legal Baron of the family. If I get married, he's in a position to take over control of the greater part of my holdings."

Joe Mauser was furious. "Well, let him! It's only money. We've got plenty. I have a few shares of Variable and we both have our dividends as Uppers, from our Inalienable Basic Shares. We can live without your Vacuum Tube Transport holdings."

She looked at him sadly. "Joe, you forget. We both belong to the organization. Any revolutionary movement needs funds. I am plowing most of my dividends into its coffers."

"Damn it! I *want* you."

She put a hand on his arm, and for the first time since he had met her, there was a demure look on her face. She cast her eyes down to where her fingers fiddled with her fork. She said, "Joe, I am not adverse to sleeping with you."

Chapter Six

Joe gaped at her.

It was not that he was an innocent. In his thirties, now, Joe had in his time bedded many a woman, most of them hot-eyed fracas-buffs anxious to put out for a man she might see the next day in action on her telly. Might even see him kill—or be killed. Frankly, he had a certain dislike of the type. But there you were. A beautiful girl offering her body, for absolutely free, and for all you knew tomorrow you might get into the dill and cop one, perhaps the final one. Don't look a gift horse in the mouth. At least, it was better than buying it. There had been others, down through the years. Indeed, he had had several serious affairs and had even considered marriage. However, his ambition had driven him. He rebelled against being tied down to a Lower or Middle wife, who might be a drag on his ever attaining Upper caste. Category Military was one of the few in which bounces in caste could be comparatively quick, if you proved yourself and received promotions. It didn't help to have a poorly-educated wife.

She said, a trifle tartly, "Don't you want me?"

"Yes, of course. I've always wanted you. Since the first time I saw you."

The thing was, Joe Mauser had never really gotten over the fact that he was in love with an Upper and that she returned his affection. He still retained that built-in awe of the born aristocrat. It was as though he was a serf courting the Duke's daughter. Did a Duchess ever eat anything as plebian as bread? Did she ever sleep on anything less than silk? Did her bowels ever move, or did she ever have to relieve her bladder? Above all, would she ever submit to sex with a lout such as himself? Joe Mauser had desired Nadine Haer as he had never desired another woman in his life, but subconsciously he had never, never really expected the day to come when he would penetrate her sexually.

She was saying, gently, "Joe, I am not a virgin. I am nearly as old as you are. I am an M.D., and I have no religious scruples, so it's not to be expected of me. I have not been...promiscuous, but I am not a virgin. One of the reasons that I am so anti-fracas is that my first...lover, to whom I was also engaged, Joe, was in the Category Military. He, I believe the term you use is *copped one*, when he was only twenty-two."

"I don't know why I should argue," Joe said, smiling at her. "How long will this hassle of yours with your brother continue?"

"The lawyers say it might remain in the courts for years. Balt will never let go of his semi-control of my holdings if he can help it, especially the voting rights. And he still remains Baron of the Haer family." She snorted disgust. "They call it People's Capitalism. Industrial Feudalism is the better term."

Through all this, they had been nibbling at their lunch. Neither had much appetite, although the food of the Swank Room was delicious. Spontaneously, both of them put down their utensils.

"When was Holland due at your place?" Joe said.

"This afternoon. Perhaps we should go."

Joe brought forth his universal credit card and put it in the table's payment slot.

He grinned at her. "That sounds good to me. Obviously, I'm anxious to get you alone."

She made a face at him. "Darling, you're so ardent," she said.

They took a hovercab out to the Haer mansion on the outskirts of the city. On the way, Joe Mauser opaqued the windows and took her, unresistingly, into his arms.

"Can't you wait until we get home?" she asked.

"No," he said, kissing her.

He was aware of the fullness of her breasts against his chest, doubly aware of the firmness of her thigh against him. He cupped one of her breasts in his hand and felt the nipple respond. Nadine Haer was all woman. They had kissed before, certainly, and often, but this was the first time he had intimately fondled her. She obviously didn't mind. He suspected that she was as keen to sleep with him as he was with her.

They pulled up before the palatial residence of the Haers. Before they could get to the door, it opened and the butler politely greeted them.

"Good afternoon, Donald," Nadine said. "I am expecting Mr. Holland. Show him in immediately."

"Yes, Doctor Haer."

Save for the usual batman during a fracas, Joe Mauser had never had a servant. It fact, he had never known of a servant in these days of automation, except in the homes of the Uppers. He didn't know, but he suspected that there were at least a dozen of them in the Haer home.

They strode toward the living room, Joe looking about him appreciatively. Admittedly, the place was furnished and decorated in the best of taste. The paintings were originals and some were obviously worth a fortune. He suspected that Nadine had done much of the decorating.

He said to her, "What's going to happen to the Uppers when this socioeconomic change of ours takes place?"

"We'll put them to work, like everybody else," she said crisply.

"And what'll happen to houses like this?"

"Why...I don't know. We'll change them to rest houses, nursing homes, something like that, I suppose."

They entered the spacious living room, Nadine saying over her shoulder, "Drink? Perhaps a cognac?"

"Fine," Joe said.

Balt Haer got up from the sofa on which he had been seated, at first unseen by them.

There was a strong family resemblance between him and Nadine. But there was something else about him. He had the aloof look of the aristocrat.

"Well," he said, "the ambitious ex-Major Joseph Mauser. The only man I have ever heard of to scheme his way up from the ranks of the Lowers to become an Upper. The Department of Categories must be out of their minds. If every Tom, Dick and . . . Joe can become a member of the Upper caste, why have castes at all?"

"Oh, come off it, Balt," Nadine said, heading for the bar. "Joe is my guest. He didn't come here to be insulted."

Joe said evenly, "Good afternoon, Baron Haer."

Balt ignored him and said to Nadine, "What did he come here for? I've wondered about the truth behind his expedition to Budapest, which resulted in his being bounced two full castes."

"I'm afraid that's a state secret, Baron," Joe said. He had no intention of allowing the other to irritate him.

"There's something unusual about the whole thing," the other said, his nostrils flaring. "With no background in diplomacy whatsoever, you are named a member of our embassy in Budapest, you go over there, and you kill a Hungarian officer in a duel, then come scurrying back after being declared persona non grata."

"I was a military attaché," Joe said mildly.

The fact of the matter was, both Joe and Nadine knew, that he had been sent to the Sov-world by Hodgson and Holland to contact the Sov underground. They wanted to be sure of what might happen if the United States of the Americas was temporarily in a state of confusion during a change in socioeconomic systems To their relief, Joe had discovered that there was an equivalent organization in the Sov-world which wished to overthrow the Communist Party, which had become as hereditary and worthless as the Uppers in the West-world.

Nadine came back with two cognacs and handed one of them to Joe. She said politely, "Drink, Balt?"

"Certainly not," he snapped. ' I don't drink with my inferiors. I came here to discuss some legal matters with you, Nadine."

She said coldly, "Who are your *inferiors*, Balt? Take up the legal problems with my lawyers. I know what you are trying to do and will fight you all the way down the line. You threw away your own inheritance, and now you want to get your hands on mine."

He was infuriated and glared from her to Joe. Joe calmly sipped at the brandy.

Balt Haer said, "I refuse to discuss this in front of a stranger." He headed for the door.

When he was gone, Joe said, "I thought your brother lived here."

"No longer," Nadine said. "He's moved to one of his clubs. I got the feeling that he didn't want me around to overhear some of his Nathan Hale Society meetings. He knows very well that I'm connected with what he calls a subversive organization."

She sat down with her drink, and he took a chair across from her. He looked down into his snifter glass.

"You know," he said thoughtfully, slowly. "I'm beginning to wonder about that attack on me in Mexico.

"How do you mean, darling?"

"What rank does your brother hold in it?"

"Why, he's the head man in Greater Washington, the National Headquarters, and a member of the National Committee."

65

"And he knows that you belong to a radical organization? Even if he didn't hate my guts, he'd probably suspect that I, too, belong. That outfit maintains a squad of goons, doesn't it?"

"Yes," she said in undisguised disgust. "They're terrible. If someone makes a public statement even mildly opposed to some aspect of People's Capitalism, they'll go around and beat him up. It's suspect that they have actually assassinated some of the more vocal opponents of the Ultra-Welfare State."

"So one of Balt's goons might have planted a directional bug in my car, and several of them might have followed me down to Mexico and waited for me to get off the beaten trail, where they could finish me off."

She pressed her elbows tightly against her sides in a gesture of feminine rejection. She said in protest, "But he's my brother, darling."

"And one of the most reactionary funkers I've ever met."

"But surely he must realize that I love you," she said. "Surely it shows."

"And he'd rather you be married to a pig, I'm an Upper now, but he doesn't really consider anyone an Upper unless he was born into the caste. For him, I'm still a Lower and a born slob."

A voice from the door said, "Am I interrupting anything?"

It was Philip Holland, Category Government, Rank Secretary, Middle-Middle. But he was much more than that. He was the secretary of Harlow Mannerheim, Minister of Foreign Affairs, alcoholic extraordinary. Philip Holland was the brains behind the throne. He did the actual work. Mannerheim, an Upper-Upper, often didn't even bother to come to his offices for weeks on end. When he did, he didn't have the vaguest idea of what was going on.

Philip Holland was about forty, physically on the slight side. He had a way of cocking his head and chuckling when he made a point, and seemed just slightly stuffy. Joe had long suspected that he had a thing going for Nadine and wasn't happy about Joe Mauser moving in. However, with Frank Hodgson, he was top man in the organization and was dedicated enough to know that Joe Mauser was a valuable ally.

Nadine said, "Phil! How are you?"

"Wizard, my dear. And you look well." He looked over at Joe. "You're back awfully soon. We expected your expedition to take a week or so."

Nadine stood and went over to the bar. "Martini?" she said, obviously knowing the other's preference.

Joe felt a twinge. Nadine had said that she wasn't a virgin. Had Phil Holland been one of her lovers? And then he felt like a cloddy. Jealousy at his age? The most sterile of all emotions.

"It's a little early, but yes," the bureaucrat said to Nadine. And then to Joe, "How did it come off?"

Joe finished his brandy and put down the snifter glass and told him in detail.

"Two hundred new members!" Holland marvelled. "And largely Middles. We need more Middles. Things are beginning to move, perhaps. However, I don't like that attack upon you."

"Neither did I," Joe said dryly. "In spite of my former profession, I loath being shot at."

Nadine had brought Holland's drink to him and sat down.

Phil Holland sipped at his Martini, then said to Joe, "Do you have any idea of who might have taken that crack at you?"

"I suspect Balt's Nathan Hale Society. He's fanatical about subversives and he accuses Nadine of being one. And, of course, I see a great deal of Nadine. He probably adds two and two together adequately, though otherwise he doesn't seem to be very astute."

"Oh, wizard!" Holland looked over at Nadine. "What do you think he thinks about *our* relationship?" he asked cynically.

"He thinks you're courting me. He's made snide remarks to that effect from time to time."

"But I'm a Middle."

"Yes, but he realizes perfectly well that if you went to the trouble of pulling a few strings, you could bounce yourself up as high as you wanted to go, even to Upper-Upper. I suspect he's mystified that you haven't."

"Couldn't be bothered," Holland chuckled.

Joe leaned forward. "Just one thing about that Mexican romp. I've reported my car stolen. They've found it bombed and with five dead men in the vicinity. It won't be long before somebody comes around to question me."

The other nodded. "Frank Hodgson, in his position in the Bureau of Investigation, can handle it. It's not a local matter and comes under his jurisdiction."

Joe said, "Wizard. One other thing. Jesus Zavala pointed out something that was interesting. His own outfit had come to the same conclusions as we have. He claims that the closer we come to our socioeconomic change the more groups will spontaneously evolve in the same direction. Some smalls, some large. They'll mushroom up all over the place."

Phil Holland thought about it. "He's probably right. And it's an idea. We're going to have to start looking for such groups. We've got to increase our speed of recruitment."

Nadine said, "The Sons of Liberty."

The two men looked at her.

She said, "I've heard of them several times. An organization that wants to make basic changes."

68

He looked over at the younger man and wound it up. "So that's how we got into the current rut, Max. We've become a nation of cloddies."

Max, looking very unhappy, got up and went over to the autobar for another beer. "What another one?" he said.

"No. I've got to keep a clear head."

Max came back, still disgruntled. He said, "Well, maybe most of us are in a rut, but what can you do? With, like you said, all this here automation, there just aren't no jobs."

Joe explained to him that work connected with production and distribution of necessities wasn't the only kinq. There was education and the sciences, such things as the space program, ecology and the environment, and the arts. How much of it Max assimilated, Joe didn't know.

The identity screen on the door buzzed. He looked over and it was Nadine, as expected. Joe got up and hurried over.

Nadine smiled brightly as she entered, "Hello, Max," she said. "Hello darling."

Max shot to his feet. "Hi, Doctor Haer," he said. "Gosh, you look all shiny."

"Thanks, Max," she said. She looked at Joe in amusement from the side of her eyes. "I feel all shiny."

"So do I," Joe said, "but I didn't know it showed. How about a drink, darling?"

"I'll have a Cooler," she said.

Max excused himself and went on into his own room, probably thinking that they wanted to be alone. He knew that they were engaged, but thus far Joe hadn't told him the wedding had been put off indefinitely. Max would have welcomed the news. He didn't like the idea of giving up his shared apartment with his friend.

Joe brought her the drink and one for himself and sat

on the couch next to her.

He shook his head in despair and said, "I've just been talking to Max about the organization. Frank Hodgson is of the opinion that we're going to have to start recruiting Lowers. They number some ninety percent of the population. It's hard for them to identify with even a Middle, not to speak of an Upper. Max was born a Low-Lower and he's now a Middle-Lower, so he's right on their level."

"Frank is undoubtedly right," Nadine said. "How did Max respond?"

"I'm not really sure, but I got the feeling that he was shocked to find that I was speaking against the government."

"Zen!" she said. "Do you mean to tell me that after all this time, after our trip to Budapest, after your expedition down into Mexico, Max didn't even know about our organization and what it stands for?"

"Evidently not. He finds the words and the concepts a little hard. After about the third sentence that he can't understand, he turns off listening."

She stared at him, frustration in her face.

"Max is above average as Low-Lowers go. But he probably had no more school than the minimum to teach him how to read and write a little, and how to add and subtract. I don't know. Possibly he can even divide—at least short division. As a kid he undoubtedly cut school as often as possible to watch the fracases on telly. And from what he's said about his home life, his parents couldn't have cared less. I doubt if he's ever read a book in his life."

She took a sip of her Cooler. "And it's your belief that he's more than average?" she asked.

Joe shook his head. "I'm in a better position than you are to know the workings of the Lower mind. I was born a Lower myself. I'm one of the few I've ever heard about that had any push, any ambition. On top of that, as a member of the Category Military, I had Lowers under me, after I'd achieved noncom and then officer rank. In short, I've associated with Lowers all of my adult life. I know them."

"Ninety percent of our population," she said in continued despair.

"Yes."

Nadine took a deep breath and finished her drink. "How did your morning's work turn out otherwise?"

"I think I've made a good contact. I don't know if you've met Freddy Soligen. I guess not. He was the telly reporter who tried to build up my image in the eyes of the fracas buffs. At any rate, he's had the dream of bettering his condition under People's Capitalism as long as I have. And he's a fighter. Ambitious. He's also one of the most experienced reporters in the Category Communications. He wants to get out of reporting the fracases. I suggested to him that possibly we could swing him into a job as a Rank Commentator, if he joined our team."

Nadine considered it, and said finally, "I don't see why not. Both Frank Hodgson and Phil Holland have close personal friends, school chums and that sort of thing, in Communications."

"Organization members?"

"No, I don't think so. Just friends, but the kind of friends you can twist an arm on, when it comes to a favor."

Joe grimaced and said, "You know, it occurs to me that in all of these months the only members of the organization I've ever met were you, Frank Hodgson, Phil Holland and General George Armstrong in Budapest, and you're all in the upper echelons of the

71

organization. I haven't met a single other member, except those new two hundred headed by Zavala down in Mexico."

She shook her head, laughed, and said, "Haven't you figured that out, Joe? We don't want anybody else to know about you. You've become our ace trouble-shooter. If you're not known, you can't be betrayed. And any subversive organization is rotten ripe for betrayal. If any Category Security or Nathan Hale Society members have infiltrated our ranks at a lower level, our plans will be ruined."

"I suppose so," he said and switching subjects. "How'd you make out today?"

"As I told you, we have an appointment with Doctor Lawrence Mitfield, the head of the Sons of Liberty. Happily, he's right here in the area. Over in the Richmond section of Greater Washington."

"I've just vaguely heard of this Sons of Liberty group. What do they stand for?"

"I don't really know. I understand that they've put out various pamphlets and that they have an under-ground newspaper. They're on the Category Security list as a subversive organization. But that doesn't mean much. You can be listed as a subversive if you prefer vanilla ice cream instead of the chocolate that Wallace Pepper, the head of the North American Bureau of Investigation, likes."

"Yeah," Joe said in resignation. "When do we go see this Doctor Mitfield?"

"Now."

Phil Holland nodded and said, "It seems to me I've heard of them myself. Have you any idea at all of how to make contact?"

She said, "As I recall, A Doctor Lawrence Mitfield is the Greater Washington head. They have various branches throughout the country."

Holland stood, having finished his drink. "All right. You two look him up and sound him out. Meanwhile, my dear, I think that I should refrain from seeing too much of you, much though I hate to say it. Your brother may get ideas as a result of our association, much as he has seemingly done with Joe, here." He looked at Joe. "As I said, we've got to speed up our recruiting, especially among those who have connections with publicity, news reporting, that sort of thing. When our day of action comes, we've got to be able to contact people wholesale. If you have any ideas, utilize them."

'I'll work on it," Joe said. "Only remember that I have damn little background or experience except in the world of the fracases."

"Okay," Holland said. "I've got to get back to the office." He smiled cynically. "And do the work of the Upper who is supposedly our Minister of Foreign Affairs."

When he was gone, Nadine stood and came over to Joe. She took his hand and said impishly, "Come along."

She seemed a different Nadine than the one he had known. Mystified, he came to his feet and let her lead him. She led him upstairs to what was obviously her bedroom. She closed the door behind her and faced him.

At this time of day? he thought. But then, who was he to argue? This was the woman he loved.

She said, demurely, "I told you that I wasn't promiscuous, and not very experienced. But I've found out one thing that men seem to like."

"So have I," he told her, reaching for her.

"Not that, silly," she said. "Something preliminary to that."

And then she did something that couldn't have surprised him more. She put her hand down to his trousers and, looking him full in the eyes, unzipped them and put her hand inside.

"Let's get to bed," he said.

Still holding onto his penis, which was rapidly swelling to full erection, she led him to the bed and sat him down.

"I know another preliminary trick," she said.

"What?"

"Men like a bit of a show," she told him. "You watch while I undress."

He sat there, still exposed, his erection complete now, while she undressed. She undressed slowly, walking up and down the room a bit, gracefully, languidly, as she removed garment after garment. Finally, she was down to silk briefs and her fairly high-heeled Etruscan-revival shoes.

She turned her back and stepped out of her undergarment. He saw the pink roundness of her magnificent buttocks, the tapered wonder of her perfect legs. She turned around, her arms relaxed along her sides, her palms toward him, as though offering herself. She smiled simply. Her pubic hair was softly red, and she was well endowed with it. Her belly was only slightly rounded, femininely so. Her breasts, as he knew from having seen her in a bathing suit, were full and set a bit wider apart than usual. The coral pink tips of the nipples had already begun to harden in anticipation of the mating to come.

"She said softly, "Do you still want me?"

He began to tear out of his own clothes, working around the hardened shaft which still protruded from his pants.

She laughed softly, stretched out on the bed. She looked absolutely wanton.

When he was as nude as she, he hurried to her side. She smiled at him mischievously—this was most certainly a different creature from the intense, dedicated Nadine Haer he thought he knew.

She laughed and said, "Let me get on top the first time. I'm as excited as you are. Besides, I'm of the belief that early in a relationship between man and woman, the woman should assert her dominance."

In this position, he could do little of the motion, but she performed enough for both of them. She came to her first orgasm almost immediately, rolled her eyes upward, and moaned in the ecstacy. Seeing her so almost brought him to his own climax, but he held it. In a moment, she increased her pace again.

Nadine came twice again. Then he could no longer hold it and began to writhe in his own agony of pleasure.

Chapter Seven

In the morning, they reluctantly separated temporarily to go about the tasks Philip Holland had set them. Nadine was going to locate Doctor Lawrence Mitfield of the Sons of Liberty, but Joe Mauser had someone else immediately in prospect. She took one of the Haer hoverlimousines into town, but Joe chose to utilize a vacuum-tube transport capsule and dial directly through to the apartment which was his destination.

He had dialed for the capsule at the terminal in Nadine's living room, and when the small light had flickered on the door of the closet-like terminal, he opened it and wedged himself into the small two-seated vehicle. He pulled the canopy over him, buckled the belt, and then dropped the pressure lever. He dialed his destination after putting his universal credit card in the payment slot.

He could feel the sinking, elevator sensation that meant his capsule was dropping to tube level to be caught up by the computerized controls and shuttled back and forth through the mazes of a vacuum-tube transport labyrinth, before being shot to his basic destination. In a few moments the capsule came to a halt, and Joe closed his eyes in anticipation. He might be an old hand in combat, but he hated that initial thrust in the vacuum-tube as much as the next man. He wondered if anybody ever got used to it.

He sank back into the pressure seat, then slowly forward again, straining against the safety belt. He was headed for the section of Greater Washington that had formerly been known as Baltimore. He arrived in minutes. The shuttling began again and he had to go through a few small traversing shots, which meant nothing so far as strain was concerned. Finally, he felt the capsule rising, and shortly a green light flashed on the dash. He undid the belt, killed the pressurizer, slid the canopy back, and said into the terminal's identity screen, "Joe Mauser, calling on Freddy Soligen."

The door opened almost immediately and Joe Mauser walked into the living room of the telly cameraman.

Freddy was heading for him, his usually cynical news broadcaster's face twisted in pleasure. He was a small man, as small and as feisty as Max Mainz. He was a Low-Middle, Category Communications, Subdivision Telly, Branch Fracas News, Rank Senior Reporter. It had been through Joe that he had gotten his bounce up from Upper-Lower to Low-Middle. He had been with Joe in the glider, covering the fracas which had led to Joe's court martial. As a reporter, not a combatant, he had won kudos while Joe had been clobbered.

He shook hands, saying, "Joe! Zen, it's good to see you. I čaught that duel you had with the Hungarian. For awhile there you were really in the dill. I thought the bulletproof Joe Mauser was going to finally cop his last one."

Joe had to laugh, even as he shook. "Bulletproof," he said. "I've got so many holes in me I look like an open door. How's it going, Freddy?"

The other led him back to the king-size telly screen in one corner, saying, "I don't know, Joe. I'm thinking of switching out of Branch Fracas News."

Joe looked at him in surprise. Freddy Soligen was the best man in his field. While the other telly cameramen were crouched in their cement pillboxes, covering a fracas in safety, Freddy was usually out there in the thick of it, getting authentic closeups right in the middle of a pickled situation. Largely, mercenaries were contemptuous of the telly cameramen, but Freddy was respected by all. When they got into the dill, Freddy was in there with them and in his time he had copped one several times. Even top men like former Field Marshal Stonewall Cogswell and General Jack Altshuler respected him.

As they approached the telly set, and Joe had been surprised to find Freddy watching it, a man in uniform stood up from the comfort chair in which he had been hidden. He was in the uniform of an unassigned Rank Private of the Category Military. Calling him a man was stretching a point. He was about seventeen, bright of eye, toothy of smile, gawky as only a teenager can be gawky. It was Sam Soligen, Freddy's son.

He said, "Hello, Major Mauser," and held out his hand somewhat hesitantly, as though an old pro like Joe Mauser might think it beneath him to shake with a tyro such as Sam Soligen in the Category Military.

"Nice to see you again, Sam," Joe said warmly. He had met the boy twice before. Joe had gone into the Category Military at the same age himself.

Freddy said, "Sit down, Joe. Could I get you a beer or something?"

"No thanks."

Joe Mauser looked at the boy. He said, "How'd it go?" He was relieved to see Sam at all. In the mercenary trade, if you lasted six months, you had a chance. Many, if not most, didn't. It was the tyros who copped their final ones, often the first time out. The veterans knew how to protect themselves, how to stay out of the dill. The longer you stayed in the Category Military, the better chance you had of surviving. You learned the ropes. Besides that, the older hands took care of each other. When the situation pickled, you sent some of the young lads in, not your old buddies. It wasn't fair, perhaps, but it was reality.

Sam said, "Aw, it was nothing. I wasn't in the dill at

78

all. All I did was march and dig entrenchments for the whole fracas. I never did get close enough to the enemy lads to shoot at them or be shot at. I've never done so much digging in my life. And as soon as we'd get one trench dug, the fighting would move to some other part of the military reservation, and they'd march us off and put us to digging again. Some fracas."

Both Joe and the boy's father laughed.

Freddy said, "Sam, you don't know when you're lucky. You got your pay, didn't you?"

"Sure, one share of Variable Basic and a bonus because our side won. But I didn't join the Category Military to dig holes."

Joe said earnestly, "Sam, if you're going to survive in your category you've got to do everything you can to stay out of pickled situations. The world is full of dead heroes, or would-be heroes. When you sign up for a fracas, try to get a job behind the lines, in logistics, in an office, or, at worst, as an officer's orderly, or even a messenger."

The boy frowned. "But you'd never get a promotion or a bounce in caste that way."

"No, but you'd stay alive."

Sam said, "Well, gee, Major, that's not the way you did it. I used to watch the fracases you were in, especially when Popper was casting them. You were getting into the dill all the time. And you got promoted all the way up to major and to Upper caste."

Joe nodded and said, "Yes, that's true, although I didn't make Low-Upper until after I was thrown out of Category Military. You see, Sam, I was ambitious. The big thing I wanted in life was to become a member of the Upper caste. For fifteen years I fought my way up, taking chances. When I finally got to the top, I found it wasn't worth it. And along the way, one by one, my closest friends copped one, the final one. I can't think of a single friend remaining since the days when I first joined up. They're either dead or retired as a result of their wounds. No, lad, if you must remain in the category, play it safe. Perhaps you won't reap much glory, whatever that is, but at least you'll live, and share by share you'll accumulate Variable stock."

"It's good advice, Son," Freddy Soligen said. "I was the same as the Major, here. I was ambitious to get bounces in caste. So I'd get right out there in the middle of a fracas and give the buffs real coverage with my camera. It's a miracle that I'm still alive. And after all these years, where am I? A Low-Middle—and it's unlikely I'll ever get any higher." He looked at Joe. "That's why I told you I was thinking of getting out of the Branch Fracas News."

Joe said, "A job's a job these days, Freddy, and with your reputation you must pull down pretty good pay. Why don't you just take it easy and stay in the pillboxes like the other reporters? You'd have your work cut out getting a position in any other field. There just aren't any jobs any more, since practically everything's become automated."

"That's part of it, too," Freddy told him. "I want to get in on the ground floor of another branch of Category Communications before half of the telly reporters in the country make the same decision. Joe, the fracas is on its way out."

Joe eyed him. "What're you talking about?"

"That last one you and I were in together with Marshal Stonewall Cogswell. I wouldn't be surprised if that wasn't the last divisional magnitude fracas ever to be fought. Haven't you noticed? Most of even the largest ones these days are usually no more than regimental magnitude, and usually smaller. A lot of them are fought between only companies of lads. The fact of the matter is that the corporations and unions

80

who fight them are bleeding themselves white. They're too damned expensive. A king-size fracas costs tens of millions of dollars to mount. Get yourself into two or three a year, and you're bankrupt."

Joe said, "Wizard, but the people, especially the Lowers, demand their bread and circuses—their dividends from their Inalienable Basic Stock and their telly fracases. They'd be up in arms if either of them were restricted."

Freddy looked at his wrist chronometer and said, "Yeah, but I didn't say they'd eliminate gore on telly, just that they're cutting back on the fracases."

Joe scowled at him in puzzlement.

The telly cameraman said, "Have you ever watched any of these new gladiator meets?" He reached out and switched on the telly set.

"Hell, no," Joe Mauser said in disgust. "And I'm not about to begin. I've seen enough blood and guts to last me the rest of my life."

"I watch them," Sam said. "They're wizard. They fight with the old weapons, like the Romans used to use."

As the scene faded in, Freddy said, "Watch this one, Joe, just for the experience. I'll tell you what I'm thinking, later."

Joe shrugged and resigned himself. He wanted to watch a couple of present day gladiators hack each other apart about as much as he wanted to have his left ear shot off.

It was all new to Joe Mauser. He had heard about these mushrooming gladiator amphitheaters, but had been contemptuous of the whole idea. In his time, he had followed a full-scale fracas on telly, usually because some close friend was involved and he was agonizing over the other's safety. He had also watched some of the major fracases simply because he wished to study the

81

tactics of some commanding officer whom he was going to be up against in the future. He had never in his life watched one for pleasure. Joe Mauser, who had for so many years dealt in death, found no pleasure in it. But he knew no one in these gladiator "games" and had no connection with them whatsoever. And he had no interest in them whatsoever. Let the drooling telly watchers follow them. It wasn't for Joe.

Onto the screen faded the arena, which turned out to be approximately the size of a bullring in a smaller Mexican or Spanish city. By the looks of the stands, Joe estimated that the amphitheater would seat about five thousand, so that all could be near enough to the combat to get a good view. Joe could make out five telly camera crews on the arena barrera. That would mean six in all, counting the camera they were now utilizing on Freddy's set. Joe imagined that there was a director in charge of deciding what camera to use at any given time. Freddy was obviously knowledgeable about the whole thing and gave a running description of what was going on. The stands were packed with yelling, cheering fans. In the sand-strewn arena were three pairs of fighters, just about to go into action.

"Secutors and Retiarius," Freddy explained. "The Retiarius are the ones with the nets. The whole thing goes back to Roman days."

The Retiarius wore no armor and carried only a tridents as a weapon. The Secutors wore helmets, carried swords and shields, and wore breastplates, and their right arms and left legs were protected with armor.

Joe said, "I wouldn't think those netmen would have much of a chance."

"It's the other way," Freddy said. "The odds are five to three against the Secutors. They're too clumsy in all

82

that armor. They can't move fast enough to avoid getting netted. Then the Retiarius steps in with his three pronged spear and finishes him off before he can get untangled."

The camera zoomed in on two of the contestants, who were beginning to square off.

Freddy said, "The netman is a celebrity. Name's Jones. The gladiator buffs love him, because he puts on a show. They call him Speedy. The other cloddy's a newcomer. Name's Rykov, I believe. He hasn't got much of a chance."

Joe took in the net. It was fringed with small lead weights, so that when it was thrown it would open to form a circle, which was very similar to a fisherman's net.

Jones, the Retiarius, waved his trident at the cheering crowd. He obviously liked his moment in the limelight. Then he came in, making tentative casts with his net. He was obviously an expert with it. Then he pretended to slip and fall, undoubtedly hoping that the swordsman would come running clumsily in, and put himself off balance.

But Rykov wasn't having any of that, thank you. He had his feet firmly planted and waited for the more active gladiator to come at him.

Jones danced around him, holding his net by one end and slinging it at the swordsman's feet, evidently hoping to have it wrap around the other's feet and legs and trip him. Then he suddenly changed his tactics and threw the net in a cast. Rykov turned it with his shield, but one of the lead pellets hit him in the left eye, partially blinding him. The Retiaruis saw his chance and, rushing in, knocked the sword out of his opponent's hand with his trident.

Both of the men ran for the sword, but the lighter

83

Retiarius got to it first, scooped it up, and tossed it into the stands. Then he returned to finish off his unarmed opponent.

The crowd roared approval.

"Rykov's had it," Freddy said.

"Holy Jumping Zen, what a way to go," Joe Mauser muttered in disgust.

But Jones made the mistake of first showing off with some fancy net casts. Rykov managed to give the trident a kick that sent it flying across the arena. The suddenly frightened Retiarius turned to run after it, but before he could get away Rykov grabbed him by his tunic. As the Retiarius went down on his knees, Rykov gave him a rabbit punch with the edge of his shield and Jones, his neck obviously broken, sank to the sands.

The mob in the stands, shocked by the sudden turnabout and the death of their champion, fell silent. Rykov looked up at them contemptuously. They began to boo him.

Joe said, "Turn the damn thing off."

"Well, there you are, Major," Freddy said. "That's what's going to take the place of the fracas. And I figure on switching over to handling one of those telly crews. Obviously, it's a damned sight safer for me than being right in the middle of the combat."

Joe said thoughtfully, "I can see where it would have advantages over the fracas from the viewpoint of the buff. In a fracas, you have no guarantee that there'll be a telly crew on the spot when some action takes place. You might sit through a whole battle and never see any of the gore and death you tuned in for. But in a fight like that, you can't miss. Those poor funkers are on lens from the moment they walk into the arena."

"There're other angles too," Freddy told him. "When a corporation or a union gets permission from the Category Military Department to fight a fracas, it costs them millions to hire mercenaries. But these gladiator bouts make money for whoever throws one. Those gladiator buffs up in the stands, who'd rather see the fighting live than on their telly sets, pay plenty for seats. Each gladiator who survives gets ten shares of Variable Basic stock, but..."

"Ten shares!" Sam said. "Holy Zen, what am I doing fighting in fracases? A Rank Private like me only gets one share. I ought to switch over."

"Didn't you see what just happened?" Joe asked. "We just saw two men fight it out and one was killed. In a fight like that you have a fifty-fifty chance of copping your final one. In a fracas, either side seldom takes more than ten percent casulties, and usually less than that. So there's only one chance in ten of getting yourself in the dill and winding up in a hospital—or in the ground."

"Well, you have to take your chances," Sam said.

"You sure do," his father growled. "That man you just saw killed, Jones, was one of the oldest hands in these gladiator fights, and he was finished off by a tyro. It's a sucker's game, Son."

The boy looked at his wrist chronometer and got up from his chair. "I gotta go," he said. He came over to Joe Mauser to shake hands. "It was nice to see you again, Major."

Joe stood and said, "We'll have to get together more often, Sam."

When young Sam was gone, Joe turned back to Freddy Soligen and reseated himself. He gestured at the telly set and said, "What in the devil's the country coming to when they allow that? The fracases were bad enough."

Freddy shrugged. "Those cloddies that fight are consenting adults. Nobody twists their arms. Basically, it's the same as the fracases. You don't have to sign up for them if you don't want to. And the pay is high. How else can somebody who was born a Lower make ten shares of Variable for a few minutes time? The government's ruled that consenting adults can participate in violence, even to the point of killing or getting killed."

"What a government!" Joe said in disgust.

Freddy Soligen looked at him, eyebrows high. "Are you talking against the government, Joe?"

"You're damn right I am."

"Well, then you're lucky you aren't talking to somebody who'd turn you over to Category Security. But if you like it or not, there's nothing you can do about it. I'm not saying that there aren't some aspects of People's Capitalism that I'd like to see changed, but there's nothing you can do about it."

"Yes, there is," Joe said grimly. "That's what I came to see you about, Freddy."

"What do you mean?"

"I came around to recruit you into an organization which has as its aim changing the present socioeconomic system."

Freddy looked at him. "What does that mean, the socio . . . whatever you said?"

"It means the government and the present way of handling production, distribution, scientific research and so forth. We want to get the country back on the tracks, back to work, back to progress."

"Oh, wizard," Freddy said with a snort. "Chum-pal, you sound as though you've gone drivel-happy."

Joe said, "Well, from what you've told me in the past, you're as much against the way things are now as I am. You started out a Lower and tried to fight your way up. You worked like a bastard and took your risks. And where are you at the tender age of some forty-odd? A Low-Middle without much chance of getting higher.

86

You've got a son you love even more than ordinarily, he's in the Category Military, and we both know what his percentages are. And all you can do is pray the kid doesn't become silly enough to switch over to the gladiator games. So, as I say, I came to recruit you to the organization to which I belong, an organization devoted to change."

"You haven't got a chance, Joe."

"Some of the biggest men in the country are with us, Freddy."

"Who?"

"I can't tell you, especially until you're in."

"Wizard," Freddy said. "What's in it for me?"

"A thought came to me when you mentioned that you were thinking of switching out of Branch Fracas News into some other branch of Category Communications. How would you like to switch to Branch News and become a Rank Commentator?"

Freddy laughed. "Yeah, and I'd like to be bounced in caste to Upper-Upper too. Rank Commentator is as high as you can get in Category Communications, Subdivision Telly."

Joe said seriously, "I told you that some of the biggest men in the country were behind this organization. I think we could swing it."

"I'll be damned. What would I have to do?"

"Probably not much at this stage of the game. We're not ready to move as yet. But when we do, we want to have people in the news media."

Freddy thought about it. He said finally, "What are some of the things you stand for? You can't just overthrow the government without something to take its place."

"Among other things, one that you've been in revolt against all of your life. The caste system. We want to do away with it. No Upper-Uppers. No more Lower-Lowers. Everybody reaches his level in society on his own merit."

It was there that Joe Mauser had made his mistake.

Freddy Soligen was not opposed to the caste system. He was simply ambitious within it. He wanted to get as high on the totem pole as he could manage and by whatever method that came within his reach. He was an opportunist of the old school. Freddy Soligen was out for Number One, Freddy Soligen, and, of course, his son, Sam. And nothing else was going to stand in his way, including friendship.

He said, carefully, "Tell me more about this organization of yours, Joe."

Chapter Eight

Joe Mauser, happy because he was in the process of making an outstanding recruit, returned to his apartment by vacuum-tube capsule. He emerged into his own living room to find Max Mainz sitting before the telly.

The little man had a plastic of beer in his hand and made a gesture of greeting to Joe. He said, "Hi, Major. Where've you been?"

Joe Mauser said, "Around." He slumped into a chair beside his roommate. "Don't tell me you've found something worth looking at on the goof-box."

Max said, "Aw, telly's not so bad. It's something to do. You can't just sit around, just doing nothing."

Joe said, looking impatiently at him, "Didn't it ever occur to you to take up some studies? You could get yourself some extra background. It might even lead to you being able to get a job."

Max took back a slug of his beer. "Why?" he said reasonably. "I got my Inalienable Basic. I got a few shares of Variable Basic now. I got it made. I don't want to be no stute. We're living high on the hog, Major."

Joe Mauser sighed. He got up and went over to the auto-bar and dialed himself a duplicate of Max's beer and came back with it.

He settled into his chair disconsolately. Phil Holland had said that they were going to have to recruit the Lowers, sooner or later. And Max Mainz was a bit more than average when it came to Lowers.

Joe said, "Max, have you ever heard of the Nathan Hale Society?"

"Sure."

Joe eyed him. "You have?"

"Sure. I just seen something about it on the telly news. They're gonna have a big rally tonight, over at Druid Hill Park. Free beer and everything."

Joe thought about it, between sips on his drink. He said, finally, "Look. How about going over and attending the rally? Find out all you can about the outfit. If they hand out any leaflets or pamphlets, or whatever, get copies of them."

Max said, "Why?"

"Because they're probably the funkers who took a crack at us down in Mexico. I want to know more about them."

"You're the boss," Max said, finishing his beer. "What'm I supposed to find out?"

"Damned if I know. Anything that you can. What makes them tick. What they stand for. Who's behind them. Who their leaders are, besides Balt Haer. That sort of thing. Anything."

They sat for awhile, staring at the goof-box as Joe had named it. There was a crime show in progress, complete with more Mayhem than had ever happened in the real world of crime. Joe had come into it in the middle and couldn't follow the plot.

Max said, "You shoulda seen what was on before this. A gladiator show. This guy Rykov . . ."

"I saw it," Joe said.

"You did?" Max was surprised. "I didn't think you looked at stuff like that."

"I usually don't. It's for empties, Max."

The ugly little man scowled. "You oughtha talk like that, Major. It's un-American. All Americans follow the fracases and the gladiator games and the phoney-fracases."

"No they don't Max," Joe sighed. "Practically nobody does except the Lowers. And especially the Low-Lowers. Vicarious violence is the need of people who have become the rejects of life. They're trying to strike back at a world that has deserted them."

"I don't know what in Zen that means but..."

Joe interrupted him impatiently, saying, "That's why I suggested that you take some courses from the computers of the Educational Category, Max. Possibly you'd learn what I just said meant."

"Aw, I told you. I don't want get to be a stute."

"Don't worry, Max; you won't."

Joe brought his transceiver from his jerkin pocket and dialed Nadine Haer. In a moment, her face faded in and immediately expressed her pleasure in seeing him.

"Darling!" she said.

He got up and went to the far end of the room, leaving Max to his sudden death show and his exaggerated mayhem.

Joe said into the transceiver, "Last night you were absolutely shameless."

Her eyes widened mockingly, and she said, "I'll never do it again."

"That remains to be seen," Joe said.

Nadine dropped the banter and said, "How did you do?"

"Pretty good, I think. I'll have to check it out with the, ah, higher-ups, but I think I've got somebody good. And you?"

"I've got an appointment with... our subject. Suppose I come by your apartment and we'll go together."

"Wizard, and... darling..."

"Yes?"

"I like shameless girls."

"I'll never be the same." Her smiling face faded from the screen.

Joe Mauser rejoined Max who had switched off the set and was scowling at his roommate.

Max said, "Major, why would these Nathan Hale

Society funkers want to finish you? And me, too, for that matter?"

"Most likely you were involved just because you were along with me," Joe told him. "They wanted to crisp me because I belong to an organization that is diametrically opposed to theirs."

"Is that what we were doing down there in Mexico? Something for this organization of yours?"

Joe sighed and said, "Didn't you hear what I said to those two hundred people in my speech at the hacienda?"

"I didn't listen too good. Too many big words. I can't concentrate too good if you use a lot of big words and the ideas are too complicated."

Joe sighed again at the little man's mental workings but said, "Briefly, Max, we think the country has gotten into a rut. Practically all progress has stopped. Over ninety percent of the population does nothing except collect their dividends from their Inalienable Basic, suck on trank, and watch their telly sets. Usually, they watch the most degrading shows they can find. We want to change that. We want to resume progress. We want to get out of the rut."

That worried Max. "You mean that you're against the government?" he said.

"That's right."

Max thought about it for awhile and then said, "This rut you say the country's in. How'd we get in it?"

"Not any one thing, Max. It was the result of several trends, including the automation and computerization of industry and even commerce. But one of the immediate things was the shortage of gold. There simply wasn't enough gold in the world to back all of the paper money the governments were printing, and you've got to have something to back paper money, something of real value, or you have galloping inflation on your hands. So our government took ten percent of the taxes from the two hundred largest corporations in the country in the form of their common stock. They put this together into what amounted to a gigantic mutual fund and called it United States Basic Common Stock and released it on all the stock markets of the world to find its level. Obviously, the stock paid good dividends. The government offered to redeem any paper dollars it had issued with shares of this stock. And they continued the tax policies and the issuing of more Common Basic until they had more than enough to back the dollar."

Max was scowling. He said, "Yeah, but that don't sound like no rut. That was a pretty good idea."

"That's just the beginning," Joe told him patiently. "At the same time the administration of relief had gone to pot. Social Security, old age pensions, unemployment insurance, veterans pensions, food stamps, and all the rest were in a state of chaos. So the government amalgamated them all and issued shares of Inalienable Basic which were backed by the U.S. Basic Common Stock to all on relief or pensions. As time went by and more and more people were on relief, the requirements to get Inalienable Basic became less and less. Supposed old age became younger and younger; unemployment insurance became forever. When those on relief began to outnumber those who worked due to automation, the government finally issued it to everybody, including children at birth. The Inalienable Basic could not be sold and reverted to the government at death."

"Well, I know all that," Max said. "Even a Low-Lower like me gets ten shares at birth."

"Ummm," Joe went on. "At the same time, the Universal Credit Card was coming in along with the Banking Data Computers. The dollar was maintained as a symbol, but in actuality all exchange was in the

93

hands of computers. You never saw the dividends from your stock; they were simply deposited to your account. Today, everyone receives the stock, but Lowers get less than Middles and Middles get less than Uppers. And that's the way the Uppers are perpetuating themselves as a class. You can no longer go broke, no matter how stupid you are. Most of them, of course, also own Variable Basic, which can be bought and sold, but which is still based on U.S. Basic Common. And some still own blocks of stock in the corporations."

Chapter Nine

Nadine Haer hated vacuum-tube capsules, so they took her hoverlimousine by automated underground ultra-highway to the Richmond area. It was noonish, and the appointment with Doctor Mitfield wasn't until one, so they located an Upper caste restaurant and had lunch.

They checked the menu, set into the table, and dialed their selections. They they leaned back in their chairs, waiting for the food to be delivered.

Joe said, "What do you know about this Doctor Mitfield?"

"Not much. He's an M.D., which probably means that he's an Upper-Middle."

"Nothing on him in the data banks? Frank Hodgson should be able to get that with his position in the Bureau of Investigation."

"He's listed as a possible subversive and a suspected member of the Sons of Liberty, which is definitely regarded to be a subversive organization."

Joe pursed his lips. "Should we be seen in his company?"

"You've got to take chances sometimes, or you'd never get anything done," she said.

"I suppose so," He grimaced and said, "You told me that your brother, Balt, knew or suspected that you belonged to a subversive organization. Are you listed in the data banks as a subversive?"

She smiled. "No."

"You think that Balt has failed to report you because you're his sister?"

"Never fear. It's not that If I was found guilty of subversion, he, as family head, would be in a position to take over my holdings in our corporation. But each time he, or any other member of the Nathan Hale Society, reports me, Frank Hodgson has the information deleted from my dossier in the data banks, which is child's play for him, but which I suspect is driving my dear brother drivel-happy."

"Does Hodgson do the same for all the other members of our outfit?"

"Yes. His position as actual head of the Bureau of Investigation is one of our strongest weapons. Category Security, and the various other witchhunters find it practically impossible to get anything on any of us. As the organization becomes larger, that's going to become more difficult. Frank would be sticking his neck out too far by trying to clean up the dossiers of tens of thousands of members."

They ate in silence for a few minutes while Joe mulled it over. 'Could Frank delete any reference to this Doctor Mitfield being connected with subversion?" Joe asked.

"I imagine so, if we find that we're kindred spirits. And all the other higher echelons of the Sons of Liberty, for that matter. But this, at best, isn't going to be as easy as your assignment down in Mexico. The Sons of Liberty is a national organization, with, I understand, local groups in at least all of the larger cities. If we sell him a bill of goods, then he, in turn, is going to have to resell it to thousands."

"Well, let's get started," he said, bringing forth his Universal Credit Card and putting it in the payment slot of the automated table.

He said, "Did you know that in Lower and Middle restaurants you have to put your credit card in the slot before the food is delivered?"

"Why, no. I've never eaten in such places. Theoretically, an Upper can enter Middle, or even Lower,

96

establishments, but in actuality you feel conspicuous. Why do they have to pay before hand?"

Joe shrugged. "Snobbery, I suppose. One more status-symbol. It is assumed that an Upper wouldn't dream of walking out on a restaurant bill. But the lower castes are suspect."

"How ridiculous," Nadine snorted as he took her arm and they headed for the door.

The cover of Dr. Lawrence Mitfield was excellent. As an M.D specializing in coronary conditions, hundreds of "patients" streamed in and out of his offices. It would have been well nigh impossible for a Category Security agent to decide who were bona fide sick people and who were members, or potential members, of the Sons of Liberty.

The reception room was crowded and presided over by a neat, overly-smiling nurse. Most such offices, these days, had automated receptionists, but evidently Doctor Mitfield was old-fashioned.

Nadine told the girl that she and Joe had an appointment. The other smiled apologetically and asked them to be seated.

When they had found places for themselves, Joe asked, "How long's it been since you practiced, Nadine?"

"Quite a while. Not since I came in with Phil and Frank. Except when father would get embroiled in one of his corporation fracases. Then I'd rally around and help with the wounded in the field hospitals. I suppose it was my conscience. It was through the Haer family that those lads had taken their wounds."

Joe laughed lightly and said, "If I had known that it would have been you who would doctor me after I'd copped one, I would have signed up with Vacuum Tube Transport more often."

"Gallantly said, dear one," Nadine told him. "But I'm glad I never had occasion to carve you up. The very thought of it makes me shiver. How often were you wounded, Joe?"

He thought about it emptily, before saying, "I can't remember. But only a half dozen times seriously."

She eyed him. "What do you mean, seriously?"

"Bad enough that I could have died if I hadn't received prompt medical treatment."

"Zen! Half a dozen times!"

He brushed it off. "That's over a period of some fifteen years, darling. On top of those, all of which kept me hospitalized for lengthy periods, I copped quite a few minor hits."

The nurse smiled brightly at them, proving she had perfect teeth, and said, "The doctor will see you now."

They filed into the office beyond, the door closing behind them.

They found a typical doctor, complete with white jacket. He was somewhere in his mid-thirties, wore old fashioned glasses, and wore his hair short. His eyes were tired, the eyes of a dedicated man who worked hard at his profession.

"Please be seated," he said in a squeaky voice that didn't live up to his appearance. He obviously assumed them to be man and wife.

Joe said, "Is there any possibility that this office might be bugged?"

"Bugged? By whom?"

"Possibly Category Security. They suspect you, you know."

Mitfield squinted quizzically at the two of them. "Yes, I know. No, the office isn't bugged. We keep up on the latest methods of surveillance of that type and take counter measures. Yes, I know they are aware of me, but they can prove nothing. Besides, I have good

98

contacts in the ranks of the Uppers to shelter me. Who are you?"

"We're two persons who are interested in the Sons of Liberty, rather than the conditions of our hearts," Nadine told him.

"I see. Then, you wish to join the Sons of Liberty?"

"Not exactly," Joe said. "We want you to join us."

"Or, perhaps," Nadine added, "for our organizations to amalgamate."

"That would depend on our being in complete agreement," the doctor said cautiously.

"Perhaps not completely, at first," Nadine said. "Just reasonable agreement. We could debate and adapt, according to which of us had the most reasonable position on this stand or that."

"How many do you number?"

Joe said, "That would come under the head of restricted information, until we discuss unification in more detail, wouldn't it?"

The doctor said, "I suppose so. What is the name of your organization?"

Nadine laughed. "We have none. We just call ourselves the organization, or the tendency, or the movement. All in the belief that this might confuse the Category Security a bit. Being unimaginative types, as security people so often are, they need a label to hang on us, though they have none. I imagine, as things develop, we'll have to assume such a label as you have when the organization becomes a mass movement."

"Thus far, you have not told me why you have contacted me."

Joe said, "Recently, a revolutionary group which had evolved separately down in Mexico City, numbering some two hundred members, joined us en masse, since they had come independently to the same beliefs we held. One of them pointed out that there must be more such groups evolving, if our position is correct. We are seeking out other sympathetic groups."

"Revolutionary group?" Doctor Mitfield said, frowning.

"In a sense. Our organization foresees an overthrow of so-called People's Capitalism and a return to progress. The nation, and indeed the world, is stagnating. We are in contact, with a similar organization in the Sov-world that wishes to overthrow the Communist Party, which has become as hereditary in its control as have the Uppers in the United States of the Americas."

"I see." The doctor still had his fingertips together. "But the Sons of Liberty is not a revolutionary organization."

Joe scowled at him. "Then what are you? We've evidently been misinformed."

The doctor said, "I suppose that in the old days we would have been called liberal, or reformist. What we're working for is a better People's Capitalism. We wish to increase production in the nation so that we can raise the incomes of the Lowers and Middle. We wish a reform of the Education Category so that higher education is available for all. Above all else, we wish to make it easier to advance in caste. It is practically impossible now for someone born into the Lower caste to be jumped to Middle. It is even more imposibble for a Middle bor—I am an Upper-Middle—to be bounced to Upper. As a result, society stagnates. We wish to declare illegal the fracases and gladiator games. We also wish to declare illegal the drug, trank. And we want more freedom of speech, and less power in the hands of the Category Security. That's our program. The Cateory Security has branded it subversive."

Nadine stood and said, "You didn't mention capable Lowers becoming Uppers."

100

"They seldom have the ability," he responded.

"So what you are really working for is the opportunity for *you* to better your position."

"Perhaps. I suppose so."

"No basic change in society, just a better opportunity for *you*. The Uppers in power keep you and your colleagues from achieving their rank and that's what you wish to change. Otherwise, the Ultra-Welfare State is fine."

Doctor Lawrence Mitfield stared at her, but didn't answer.

Joe had stood, too. He said, "There's just one other example that possibly pertains. It's been said that a tiger will defend his whiskers as ferociously as he will his life."

"I don't believe I understand," Mitfield said impatiently.

"The Uppers will fight your attempts to merely make mild reforms in People's Capitalism as hard as they will our attempts to completely overthrow the system. You're not going to win any medals by being conservative in your demands."

"Perhaps. But that is not the way we see it."

Joe gave up. He and Nadine, without further words, left the office and made their way down to her hoverlimousine.

When they had seated themselves, preparatory to dialing their destination, he said, "So, we've been slapped in the face twice today. The Lowers, as represented by Max, are too stupid, or too satisfied with their lot, to want to change People's Capitalism. And the Middles, as represented by the Sons of Liberty, are desirous only of making it easier for themselves to become Uppers."

"Yes," she sighed. "Let's face reality, Joe. Most of those who belong to our organization are Uppers with a sprinkling of Upper-Middles. It's the most fantastic revolutionary organization that's ever been known. A segment of the ruling class that is trying to overthrow its own power."

"Yeah," he said gloomily. "Nobody wants a revolution except those who will profit least by it."

She said, "Just a minute. That car that just passed us, the hovercab."

"What about it?"

"I'm sure the man in it was Paul Warren."

"Lieutenant Colonel Paul Warren, Category Military? I've fought on the same side with him a few times. He's usually a member of Stonewall Cogswell's permanent staff."

"He's also my brother Balt's right hand man in the Nathan Hale Society."

"Oh, oh," Joe said. "That's not so good. He not only saw us together but most likely saw us coming out of the building which houses Mitfield's offices."

Chapter Ten

Max Mainz was having himself a time. The Nathan Hale Society rally was being held in Druid Hill Park on the outskirts of Greater Washington and in the area once known as Baltimore. It was a pleasant setting, and some of the Society's workers had erected a speaker's stand, well decked with American flags and pennants with such organizational slogans as *I Only Regret That I Have But One Life To Lose For My Country*, and *My Country, May She Always Be Right, But My Country Right Or Wrong*.

Max arrived early in the proceedings in the mid-afternoon, one of the first outsiders on the scene. Stands had been set up to one side, supplying the promised free beer and others with piles of Society leaflets and pamphlets on them. Members of the organization went about distributing other leaflets. Most of them wore blue shirts with a red rattlesnake sewed on above the left breast. Under the snake was stitched in heavy white thread, *Don't Tread On Me*.

Max got himself a mug of the beer and then went over to the literature stands and took one of each of the free leaflets and pamphlets. There was a plenty of them. On the face of it, the Nathan Hale Society was not hard up for funds.

He sat on an empty steel beer barrel and went through the pamphlets, once lightly. Largely, they were devoted to extolling People's Capitalism and the Ultra-Welfare State, the fact that everybody was provided for; food, clothing, shelter, education, medicine, even entertainment. The fact that never before in history had so many had so much. And on and on. Some of the material was devoted to all but hysterical attacks on anyone opposed to People's Capitalism. They were reviled as anarchists, subversives, socialists, communists, traitors, mental cases, homosexuals and dope fiends. Max wondered vaguely how it would be possible to be all of these things at once. There was even the dark suggestion that most opponents of the present laudable socioeconomic system were of races other than Caucasian and largely composed of followers of other religious sects than the government approved United Temple, of Category Religion.

Some of the reading material Max Mainz had a bit of trouble with. He was not a good reader. Who needed to read in these days of telly? But largely the free literature was aimed at people like him. In other words, the Lowers. You didn't need much of an education to follow it. It was largely slogans and cartoons. He suspected that they had more advanced stuff for the Middles and Uppers.

That brought something to mind and he looked around. As always, there was segregation. Most of the blue shirts were doing what work was involved in holding the rally. They were the ones dispensing the free beer, handing out the leaflets, making last minute arrangements on the speaker's stand. About fifty of them, billy clubs in hand, stood about the entries, through which attendants of the rally were beginning to stream. Otherwise, the area where the meeting was scheduled was roped off.

"Who the Zen they figure on slugging with those clubs?" Max muttered to himself.

The blue shirts, he decided, were most likely Lowers and probably Low-Lowers to boot. Their clothes, other than their blue shirts, would suggest that. He looked about some more, trying to locate some Middles. He thought that he could distinguish a few. Some of them wore the Society shirt and were officering the Lowers and giving directions. There didn't seem to be many Middles in the group.

He looked farther. To the right of the speaker's stand were a small group of tables and a cluster of folding chairs. The tables were covered with snowy linen and with a lavish repast, on the order of a buffet. There were a few blue-shirted Lowers going about serving, or standing behind the tables, pouring champagne and other drinkables. But largely, those in the vicinity were, by their clothing, Uppers. None of them wore the Society shirt. Quite a few, but far from all, wore uniforms of the Category Military. Lieutenant Colonel was the lowest rank. Come to think of it, Max couldn't remember ever having seen an Upper with lower rank that that.

There were women about the cluster of tables, about half as many as the men. Some kind of a women's auxiliary, Max assumed. But they, too, had no particular Society dress or emblem. They were dressed in the very latest, held champagne glasses in their soft hands, and chatted with the men.

In spite of the fact that this was a rally open to the public, Max Mainz knew well that if he walked up to those Upper tables and asked for a drink, a sandwich, or whatever, that he'd be given at the very least, a cold, aloof stare.

"Well," he told himself, under his breath. "I know bettern to try." Max was well aware of the protocol in the caste system of People's Capitalism.

Not even the prospect of free beer and trank had brought out a crowd large enough to fill the rope enclosure to anything like its capacity. Most Lowers preferred trank to beer anyway, and it was government-subsidized to the point that it was nearly free. And the shows you could watch on telly were probably a damn sight more entertaining than this was proving to be. There wasn't always a fracas in progress, of course, but there was always an abundance of reruns of old classic scraps, especially those that had provided a more than usual amount of close-ups of gore and death. Some buffs even bought cassettes of the classics and would rerun them over and over. And then there were the phoney-fracases, which were no more than what amounted to movies. They were gorier than in the old days, but less realistic.

Max wandered around a bit, beer mug in hand. The rally committee had brought in a hovertruck with a six-man band in it. The Society was certainly sparing no resources to put this over. The band started blaring martial and patriotic music, something about blessing America. Max decided that the Nathan Hale Society particularly stressed early American history, what with such slogans as *My Country Right Or Wrong* and *Don't Tread On Me*, and calling their bully-boys Minutemen. Now the band even swung into *Yankee Doodle*.

Several of the Uppers who had been gathered around the exclusive tables began to file up onto the speaker's stand and take folding chairs there. It was beginning to get slightly dark, and some of the Minutemen who were acting as guards with their billy clubs, began lighting torches. It had been decided that firelight was more inspiring.

Max refilled his beer mug again and sauntered up to an advantageous position.

The chairman began, "Fellow patriotic Americans, fellow benefactors of our glorious system, People's Capitalism..." He paused at that point, obviously for applause.

He went on to introduce the first speaker. Max missed the name and title, but it was some official connected with Category Security. It would appear

106

that he was some pretty high mucky-muck. And for the first time Max noted two telly trucks, grinding away with their cameras. Must be good lenses to be able to work in this light, Max decided. And the Society must have good connections to get the coverage. He wondered whether or not Joe Mauser was tuned in.

He was worried about Joe Mauser and that outfit he'd gotten himself tied up with. Max was still of the opinion that you shouldn't say anything against the government. Perhaps, after a while Joe Mauser would tire of all this subversive jetsam and settle down to enjoying life. Hell, between them they not only had Max's shares of Inalienable and Variable Basic but Joe's as well. Plenty to start really living it up, particularly since Joe was a Low-Upper. Max wished that Nadine Haer wasn't on the scene. He liked her well enough, but was afraid that when she married Joe there wouldn't be much room in his life for Max. Well, maybe Max could become his chauffeur, or some other kind of flunky. He'd once been in Doctor Haer's lavish home. She had a whole mess of various kinds of servants.

The speaker was going on and on, largely about subversives and how every patriotic citizen should cooperate with Category Security in bringing them to justice. He darkly hinted at the same facts that had surfaced in the leaflets and pamphlets. The malcontents were foreigners, atheists, and worse. Some of them were undoubtedly agents of the Sov-world who infiltrated into the country to overthrow People's Capitalism and the Ultra-Welfare State, so that the Sov-world could dominate all Earth.

At this point, the Middle standing next to Max Mainz laughed aloud. A silence fell. And the speaker stared down through the poor torch-supplied, light. He called in a threatening voice, "What's so damned funny?"

And the voice called back, "Sorry, it's bad manners

107

to laugh at somebody who's gone drivel-happy and obviously needs mental therapy."

Suddenly, two of the Minutemen appeared. The man in the audience tried to turn and run, but the minutemen clubbed him. He hunched over and attempted to cover his head with his arms, but nobody came to his aid. All surrounding him fell back hurriedly, and he was beaten down. The two Minutemen grabbed him up by the arms and hustled him away.

Max hadn't moved.

A voice next to him said ominously, "He a friend of yours?"

Max looked at the speaker, another Minuteman. And then recognized him as the tough-looking committeeman who had borne leaflets earlier. He had called himself Jerry. He bore a billy club now.

"Zen, no!" Max said, his tone aggrieved. "You never hear me saying nothing against the government and none of its officials. That funker just happened to be standing next to me. I never seen him before. He deserved just what he got."

The speaker went on.

Although he remained to the bitter end, Max's attention had drifted astray early in the game. In the first ten minutes, the first speaker had covered everything the Nathan Hale Society believed in. The Society stood for the United States of the Americas, particularly those northern states once called the United States, Alaska, and Canada. It was forthrightly opposed to subversives, foreigners, others than Caucasians, atheists, and espionage agents from the Sovworld and the Neut-world.

When the last speaker had called for questions from the audience, there were none. He returned to his place and there was scattered applause, largely from the Minutemen. Max made his way closer to the stand and found that Jerry had been correct. A table had been set up there with a stack of membership blanks. A half a dozen or so applicants were lined up before it. Two Uppers were seated behind, one of them in the uniform of a colonel, the other in mufti.

Max recognized the civilian. It was Baron Balt Haer, brother of Doctor Nadine Haer, Max's first inclination was to turn and leave, but he decided against it. The Baron wouldn't recognize him as one of Joe Mauser's friends.

When his turn came, Max stepped up before the head of the Haer family and came to attention. The other looked up and smiled as encouraging a smile as he was capable of when dealing with his underlings.

He said, "You wish to join the Nathan Hale Society?"

"Yes, sir!" Max said crisply.

"Name, category, rank, and caste status, please."

"Max Mainz, Category Military, Rank Private, Middle-Lower."

"Category Military, eh? Good, we don't get nearly enough applicants from the Category Military." Balt Haer frowned. "Haven't I seen you somewhere before?"

Max was worried because Balt seemed to have an uncanny memory. He had seen him only once in the past. He had been in a line before the offices of Vacuum Tube Transport when they had been recruiting for their fracas with Continental Hovercraft to be held on the Catskill Military Reservation. Max had gotten into a scrap with three larger men who were trying to take his place in the line. Joe Mauser had come to his rescue, and the fight was on in earnest until Balt Haer, a colonel at the time, had come up and put an end to it. It had been the beginning of Haer's run-in with Joe Mauser, who was then a captain. But it was unbelievable that he would remember Max.

Max said, "Yes, sir. I fought on your side in that there fracas with Continental Hovercraft."

"Oh, yes," Haer looked vague. "It must have been there. Glad to have you with us, Mainz. Just sign this paper here and give us your identification number, so that we can check out your Category Security dossier. Then come to headquarters Saturday night and we'll finish processing you. Since you're Category Military, you'll probably want to join the Minutemen."

"Yes, sir," Max said sincerely. "If there's any dill I want to be in on it."

"Good man!" Balt Haer handed over a stylo and while Max was signing up, said, "Next."

That business about the checking of his dossier set Max back a bit. Theoretically, nobody except proper government officals were in a position to examine a citizen's Category Security dossier. And the Nathan Hale Society, while proclaiming its ultra-patriotism, was by no means connected with the government, and certainly not with Category Security. He wondered what might be in his dossier that could arouse the suspicions of Baron Balt Haer. He had no way of finding out. Citizens of the United States of the Americas were not given access to their secretly compiled Security dossiers.

Chapter Eleven

Joe Mauser was having one of his not uncommon nightmares. Nadine Haer, as a doctor herself, had suggested that he take the problem to a psychiatrist, but thus far he hadn't been able to bring himself to it. He was prejudiced against psychiatrists and was against admitting that psychiatry was necessary in his case. Others might be drivel-happy, as the expression went these days, but not Joe Mauser.

The dream was about a full divisional magnitude fracas that had been fought on the same Catskill Military Reservation that many years later was to prove his Waterloo. It was between Lockheed-Cessna and Douglas-Boeing and the issue had been some huge government contract. Joe had never gotten a very clear picture of what they were fighting about. That wasn't his interest. He was a mercenary and his interests were first, staying alive, second, projecting himself well enough that it would lead to, ideally, a bounce in caste from High-Lower to at least Low-Middle, and, three, that his side, Lockheed-Cessna, would win so that he would get not only the three shares of Variable Basic that were coming to him, win or lose, but a bonus as well. They almost always gave you a bonus if your side won.

General "Bitter Dave" Langenscheidt was commanding Douglas-Boeing, and it was well known among the fracas-buffs that there was a considerable grudge between Bitter Dave and Stonewall Cogswell, who was commanding the right flank of the Lockheed-Cessna forces. and who was to win his Marshal's baton as a result of this battle. Joe Mauser was fighting under him as an infantry second lieutenant, a shavetail. And so was Jim Hawkins, his comrade-in-arms for many years.

The Category Military Department had given the two corporations permission for a maximum of one month to fight it out. If one side or the other didn't win in that period of time, the fracas would terminate and a court of senior officers of the Department would rule on who had won, or if it was a draw.

For the first three weeks, Stonewall Cogswell's brilliant tactics had seen them through to what seemed like certain victory. Langenscheidt's regiments had been backed up, until finally he set his men to building defensive trenches near the Catskill town of Lake Hill. Or, more correctly, what had once been a small town; it had been shelled into ruin long since.

Through sheer bad luck, the company to which Joe and Jim Hawkins belonged had taken more than their share of the dill. Over and over they had been thrown into the heaviest action. Stonewall Cogswell, knowing full well that they were his most experienced veterans, had used them as storm troops. Thus Joe and Jim knew with certainty that they'd go in again in the morning, when they applied to the general for a one-night pass in nearby Kingston, a city of some twenty-five thousand right on the edge of the military reservation.

It was an unusual request. Passes were seldom granted in the middle of a fracas. However, Jim Hawkins and Joe Mauser had been in almost continuous combat for three weeks and had another week of it to go.

They stood before General Cogswell's portable military desk in his field headquarters. He was a smallish man, but he had a strikingly strong face and a strong build. His voice was clipped and clear and had a ring of command, suggesting that he had given many an order and fully expected them to be carried out.

He said, "Gentlemen, my apologies for drawing

upon you and your lads beyond the call of duty to such an extent over the past weeks. However, we go into the attack at first dawn."

"Yes, sir," Jim said.

Cogswell looked from him to Joe, his face a bit testy. He said, "Do you think you can be back with your lads by that time—and sober?"

"Yes, sir," Joe said.

"I hope so, gentlemen. In view of your gallantry in the past three weeks, I have already made a note to recommend your promotions upon the conclusion of this fracas. I hope you do nothing to alter my thinking. One night pass granted. Notify the major at the desk out front."

"Yes, sir. Thank you, sir," they said in unison, saluting. He was already back at his field maps. He looked infinitely weary. Like Napoleon, it was said that he could get by with two hours sleep a night when involved in a battle.

Outside, passes in hand, they looked at each other jubilantly.

"Old chum-pal," Jim said happily, "we're in business. I need a drink almost as badly as I need to breathe."

"Second the motion," Joe said. "Let's see if we can liberate a couple of horses from some of the cavalry lads."

They borrowed the horses from two of Jack Alshuler's junior officers, who were openly envious at their Kingston leave. However, this had been a fracas in which the brunt had been thrown on the infantry, not the horse. And General Alshuler's Heavy Cavalry had largely spent their time sitting around, or going on scouts. It wouldn't have done to refuse the loan to two men who had been in the dill in the last days.

They headed for Kingston at a gallop, conscious of every elapsing minute.

Jim said, "First dawn attack, eh? Old Stonewall sounds as though he's trying to wind it up. I wonder if he figures on a frontal attack."

"That's all we need," Joe said. "But you know Cogswell. He never orders a frontal assault on a strong point, unless the other lads are punch drunk."

Jim looked over at him as they rode stirrup to stirrup. "Yeah," he said sourly, "but this is different, this time. Stonewall Cogswell and Bitter Dave Langenscheidt hate each other's guts. It's something you seldom see in Category Military. Mercenaries are philosophical about the way they make their living. One day you're up against a lad. The next month you might be on the same side he is. In between fracases, we're a tightly-knit club. If some lad is down on his luck, there's nobody quicker than a mercenary to chip in, even though a couple of months later they might be shooting at each other. But that's not the way it is with Cogswell and Langen-scheidt. Go into some officer's club, between fracases, and they can be seen in the same room. The temperature goes up several degrees. Neither looks at each other. Neither leaves. But you can feel it all over the room."

Joe said, "Can't we get any more speed out of these plugs? What the hell's that got to do with tomorrow? Everybody knows they hate each other's guts."

"What it's got to do is this. They've fought three times: this is the fourth. They've never been on the same side and aren't ever about to be. The first three times, Stonewall had taken Bitter Dave, in spite of the fact that Langenscheidt is one of the best general officers going. This time, Cogswell really wants to clobber him, really finish him off to the point where Bitter Dave will be considered a has-been. And he sees his chance for a real debacle. He's only got one week to go. Then the Category Military Department might even call it a draw. Some of those early skirmishes came out with Bitter Dave's lads looking pretty good. No, you can bet that Old Stonewall isn't thinking as coolly as usual—and it scares me."

"Oh, great," Joe growled. "Just wizard. It's all we need. After getting through three weeks of this, to get in the dill and cop one tomorrow!"

Jim said, "Same deal as always? If one of us takes a hit the other splits any additional hospital costs, fifty-fifty?"

"Same deal. This Lockheed-Cessna Corporation has a bad reputation for taking care of its casualties. The funkers put up just enough medico money to meet the minimum requirements of the Category Military Department; then you're on your own, and if you've copped a bad one that lays you up for over a month, you pony up."

They were on the outskirts of Kingston. The town on the Hudson River was the staging area of the Lockheed-Cessna element, as Catskill, some thirty miles to the north and also on the river, was headquarters of the Douglas-Boeing. This late afternoon, the town was jumping. Besides the multitude of uniformed officers and lads connected with the logistics of getting munitions and other supplies into the Military Reservation and to General Cogswell, Kingston was overflowing with fracas buffs. Undoubtedly, during the day they glued themselves to telly sets, but during the night they poured out onto the streets and into the bars, restaurants, and nightclubs.

It was a phenomenon Jim and Joe were thoroughly acquainted with. Immediately before a fracas there was a carnival atmosphere in such towns as Kingston and Catskill. The fracas-buffs turned up en masse to meet and associate with their heroes. It was practically impossible for a mercenary of any rank to buy a drink for himself. And it was practically impossible not to get laid. The fans were ultra-conscious of the fact that these soldiers would soon be in action, battling before the telly lenses, being wounded, or even killed.

The two lieutenants headed for the Hofbrau Bar, their favorite. They had to zig-zag down the street, in between the horse-drawn wagons that were hauling supplies of food and ammunition to Stonewall's division. Internal-combustion trucks were ruled off a military reservation when a fracas was in progress.

They hitched their horses to the rack before the Hofbrau, noting there were only three other animals there. Only a few of Cogswell's officers were in town, undoubtedly on business for the general.

Jim chortled, "I'm going to start off with a John Brown's Body." He walked over to the bar.

Joe climbed up on the stool beside him and said, "You remember what the general said, Back by dawn—and sober."

"Yeah," Jim told him with a wicked grin. "I feel like Cinderella. However, look at these." He held out a hand which contained two pills. "Sober-ups," he said.

Joe groaned. "They're worse than the hangover."

"But sometimes necessary. You get the whole hangover compressed into a few minutes "

"As though I didn't know," Joe said. He ordered the drinks.

Joe and Jim looked about. There were three of their fellow Lockheed-Cessna officers in a booth, but Joe and Jim recognized none of them. Undoubtedly, they were in logistics, not infantry. Otherwise, the room was full of civilians, some of whom already looked as though they were drenched. They'd probably been drinking all day while stationed in front of their telly screens.

A girl came over to Joe's right, another to Jim's left.

The girl near Joe, a plumpish, kittenish-looking blonde, whose name he was later to forget in short order, said, "Can I buy you a drink, Joe Mauser?"

Joe looked at her questioningly.

She said, "I've been watching you all week. I've been here a week now. It's the most exciting fracas I've ever seen. It's wizard. You've been in the dill a dozen times."

Meanwhile, Jim was having a conversation with his vivacious brunette, an Italian girl by the looks of her, and quite small.

The drinks had arrived and the bartender put them down and then looked at the two girls and then at Joe and Jim.

"They're with us," Jim said.

"They're with anybody," the bartender said in negation. "Anybody in a uniform." He walked off.

Joe said to his blonde, "I'll buy you one."

"Oh, no, it's on me," she said quickly. "I want to be able to tell my friends that I bought a drink for Lieutenant Joe Mauser."

She had a glass already in her hand, and she climbed up on the stool next to Joe. "In fact," she said, "I'd like to be able to tell them that I got drenched with Joe Mauser."

Joe looked at Jim Hawkins and said, "Do we want company on this binge of ours?" He should have known better than to ask. Jim Hawkins was one of the horniest men he'd ever met.

Jim didn't even return the look. He kept his eyes on his brunette and said, "I don't know about you, but I just fell in love. Love at first sight, they call it."

His girl giggled.

Joe sent his eyes down to the bartender and called to him, "Four more John Brown's Bodies."

The bartender shrugged resignation and began assembling the multi-ingredients for the drinks.

They left the Hofbrau Bar and went to the Continental Room for the floorshow. Then they left the Continental and went to the Woodstock Bar with its pseudo-artistic atmosphere. The real Woodstock, the former art colony up in the foothills of Mt. Overlook, was now a burnt-out victim of the fracases. Joe and Jim had ridden through it on the way down from the Lake Hill area where the action was being joined.

Jim said, "Drinking like this is too expensive. We should get a bottle and go off to ourselves."

His vivacious brunette said quickly. "We have a room, Lieutenant Jim."

"A room?"

Joe's blonde said hurriedly, "We reserved it six months in advance, as soon as we heard that this fracas was scheduled. We had to pay triple rates—but it has two beds." These were the ones who would give practically anything to hold Joe or Jim, or any other mercenary, in their arms the night before they were to see them in the dill the following day. To see them either kill others, preferably in profusion...or to die themselves. Yes, these two fracas-buffs were typical.

But Joe and Jim were already so far gone that having sex in beds side by side meant nothing to them. Down through the ages, the niceties had meant little to warriors who knew that on the morrow they would very possibly cop the last one. Who worries about anything—including VD—when in the morning you would very possibly cop the last one?

Joe said, at one point, after a bout, "Hey, Jim. Watch the time. We've got to be back before dawn."

Jim was resting, too, smoking a cigarette, and letting the ashes drop to the floor beside him. "I'm watching it," he said. He reached down and picked up the glass he had on the floor too. How he kept from dropping ashes into his drink was a mystery, since he was as drenched as Joe.

118

The brunette said sleepily, sex-satiated, "What happens tomorrow?"

Even in his alcoholic condition, Joe tightened. He said, "Nothing." Espionage was not unknown when rival corporations were in a fracas.

His blonde said, "How come you two infantry officers got a pass, right in the middle of everything?"

Jim had also been alerted. He said, "We've got a special in with Stonewall Cogswell. He loves us. Nothing exciting is going on, so he gave us some time off."

The brunette giggled. "It's always fun to have some inside information," she said. "Then you have something to watch for on the telly the next day."

"I'll bet," Joe said. "Like what?"

The blonde snuggled up against him, and she was a bit too lush for his tastes. She said, "Well, actually, we're Lockheed-Cessna fans, but yesterday we went up to Catskill, just to look around. We ran into the two cutest Rank Privates. They were drivers. They were darling, but just privates, not lieutenants like you two gentlemen. They were trying to be impressive, but we knew they'd only been in a few fracases."

"So how did they try to impress you?" Joe said.

"Oh, you know. They told us how important what they were hauling was."

Jim grunted. "Bully beef? Extra rounds of mortar shells?"

And his brunette said, "Oh, no. They were hurrying in a lot of *mitrailleuse* and ammunition for them."

Joe said, "What in the hell's a *mitrailleuse*?"

The brunette said, "We didn't know either. But they looked important, and kind of drenched, too. Looked like a small machine-gun."

Jim propped himself up on an elbow. "Whatd'ya mean a small machine-gun? There is no small machine-gun allowed in the fracases."

119

"Well, from what Johnny, or whatever his name was, said, it's one that one man can carry."

Jim said, "That's silly. The smallest machine-gun allowed in the fracases is the Maxim. Ideally, it takes a ten-man crew, including the ammunition carriers, of course."

"Well, from what he said, one man can use it and maybe another to carry the extra pans for him."

"What pans?" Joe snapped.

The girl was nonplused. "I think he meant the ammunition came in circular pans, like he called them. You know, not very big caliber like the Maxim or a Gatling gun. That's almost like a cannon. I've seen them in several fracases."

"So have I," Joe said grimly. He, too, was on an elbow now, and looked over at Jim. He said, "Ringing in new equipment in the last week of a fracas?"

Jim said, "There's nothing in the rules against it. It just doesn't happen very often. Usually when you go into a fracas you've already got everything you plan to use on hand. But there's nothing against it."

Joe said, "There weren't any light, portable machine-guns in use before the year 1900."

"That's what I thought," Jim said.

But the brunette said, "They're French. Johnny said that General Langenscheidt had found out that the French used them in the Franco-Prussian War, or whatever the name of that old fracas was, way back in 1871."

Jim and Joe were suddenly on their feet, stark naked.

Joe said to the blonde, "You mean to tell me Bitter Dave has been bringing in highly portable machine-guns so handy that if he had a thousand men, five hundred of them could be so armed?"

The cuddly blonde was taken aback. "Well, that was what Johnny was bragging."

120

"And we're scheduled to storm those trenches in the morning," Jim said.

The two men began to put on their clothing, both breathing deeply. They ignored the two girls, who were wide-eyed.

Jim said, "We've got to get to Cogswell in time to call off the charge."

Joe agonized, "What're we going to get to him with? The fact that two mopsies told us something that's impossible?"

"You oughtn't to call us mopsies," the brunette protested indignantly. "We paid every cent that was paid tonight."

"Shut up," Jim said to her, staring at Joe. "What'd you plan on doing?"

Joe looked at his wrist chronometer. "We'll separate and go out on the streets. We'll collar every mercenary we see and ask him if he's heard anything about Langenscheidt ringing in new French light machine-guns. We'll go into every bar that's still open and ask the bartenders if they've overheard any conversations to that extent. We'll promise them ten shares of Variable Basic if they can come up with any information."

Jim glared at him. "Where in the name of Holy Jumping Zen would we get ten shares of Variable?"

"If there is such information," Joe said, "the general would get Lockheed-Cessna to pony it up. At this point, screw it. Just promise. Let's go, Jim."

Chapter Twelve

At that stage of the nightmare, Joe Mauser, deeply asleep, broke into a sweat.

He and Jim had split up and made their desperate attempt to get more information. It wasn't forthcoming. They had considered going up to Catskill and nosing around, but they had no time for that. In their Lockheed-Cessna uniforms they would have stood out like a couple of elephants in a violet patch; they simply didn't have the time to find and switch to mufti.

They drew a blank, got back to their horses, and headed for Lake Hill as fast as they could spur their animals. Dawn was breaking. Up ahead, they could see and hear Stonewall Cogswell's initiating barrage. He was shelling the enemy entrenchments, preliminary to ordering the final charge.

Joe doubted the effectiveness of the barrage. General Langenscheidt was well dug in with the remainder of his shattered troops. When they arrived on the scene, Jim spurred on to rejoin their commands. It only needed one of them to report to Cogswell. Joe took on that duty. The general was deep in scurrying officers, scurrying orderlies, and scurrying aides. Joe had difficulty getting through. Colonel Paul Warren, one of the aides, as harassed as his commanding officer, finally got him in, when Joe's urgency became evident.

Joe came to the salute before a grim-faced Stonewall Cogswell, who looked as though he hadn't had a moment's sleep since Joe had seen him last. His face was gray with exhaustion.

"Why in the hell aren't you with your men, Lieutenant?" he said. "You were scheduled to be back here at first dawn. Your lads are to go in on the first wave. We're trying to soften up Bitter Dave before the assault."

"Yes, sir," Joe said. "We heard a rumor in Kingston and were trying to trace it down."

"What do you mean a rumor?" Cogswell snapped. "You sound to me as though you're drenched and are trying to use an alibi."

Joe then realized that he and Jim had forgotten to take the Sober-ups. His face was probably flushed and his voice uneven. He said, desperately, "Sir, we heard that Bitter Dave was bringing in large numbers of *mitrailleuse.*"

"What in the name of the ever jumping Zen is, or are, *mitrailleuse*? You're not making much sense, Mauser."

Joe said desperately, "If my French is correct, sir, the word means grapeshooter, or, more accurately, grape-shot shooter. In short, a small caliber machine-gun. What we heard is that they were highly portable. That one man could carry and operate one, preferably, but not necessarily, with another to carry extra pans. They evidently operate from a pan, rather than a belt. Makes them more portable, of course. It takes a whole crew to man even a Maxim and ..."

"I know the workings of the Maxim, Lieutenant," Cogswell said coldly. "Now rejoin your lads." He added ominously, "And you and Lieutenant Hawkins can forget what I said yesterday afternoon about a recommendation for promotion. You are both late in returning from your leave and obviously drenched."

Joe saluted and said, "Yes, sir." He did an about-face and left the tent.

Outside, his emotions were mixed, even after he had mounted his horse and taken off for the front. The withdrawing of the promised promotion was a blow, but at least the rumor of the machine-gun was scotched by Cogswell. General Stonewall Cogswell was the best man in the world of the Category Military. If he said that they were not going to face the mitrailleuse in the storming of Langenscheidt's trenches, he was probably right.

The Lockheed-Cessna infantry forces were largely drawn up in a wood below the crest where the Boeing-Douglas troops had dug in so deeply. They had scooped out their own temporary foxholes and were waiting philosophically while Cogswell's field artillery blasted the trenches above. They were in no hurry whatsoever for the barrage to end. Every shell fired was another guarantee that when they advanced, the situation wouldn't pickle for them. It looked as though the fracas was all but over, and that they'd survive and earn their bonus. Nevertheless, their faces were pale and wan. One never becomes a veteran of such experience by going into a frontal assault without being both wan and pale.

Joe located Jim Hawkins and dropped down beside him, seeking cover from whatever reply the Boeing-Douglas outfit might be making to Cogswell's barrage. Bitter Dave's artillery had been largely knocked out. He said, "False alarm. Old Stonewall says it's an impossibility. What's the word?"

Jim sighed in relief and said, "That's good news. Major Hallidat came by a few minutes ago. The minute the barrage ends, you and your lads go in first. We back you up, in a second wave. Sergeant Hix is over there near the fence. I told him that you'd be along shortly."

Joe crawled back again to Jim's foxhole. He said, "Maybe by tomorrow this whole thing will be over. We could go back and look up those two mopsies."

"You dreamer," Jim laughed at him. "By this time, they've already lined up a couple of other funkers."

The shelling ended suddenly, the guns falling silent simultaneously.

"This is it," Joe said, coming to his feet. He held up an arm and shouted, "Okay, lads, let's go. This is a milk run. It's all over. We can get our bonuses!"

"Ha!" Jim growled, too low to be heard by the Rank Privates. "It's never all over. Zen! My head. Good luck, Joe. If you cop one in this advance, I'll never forgive you. I need a drinking chum-pal tonight to help me take a hair of the dog that bit me."

"It's a milk run," Joe repeated. "Like we said last night, the general never orders a head on assault until the enemy's already practically helpless."

He drug his .44 Smith & Wesson from its holster and waved it above his head, in an attempt to be dramatic. He pointed his left hand at the entrenchments on the hill above and was the first to scramble into the open field. He yelled, "Up and at 'em, lads! Take 'em prisoners if at all possible. You might be in the dill yourselves some day and prefer to be taken prisoner, rather than copping one. And those lads up there are in the dill!"

There was a concrete pillbox only a few yards to the side, and he could make out the light-reflecting lenses as the cameramen ground away.

"Bastards," he muttered bitterly, even as he went into a slow run, his lads rising up behind him to left and right, and going into the slow, crouching trot he had assumed. They were armed with the Spanish-American War 45-70 caliber Springfield, low on velocity but carrying an ultra-heavy slug. The enemy, he knew, bore Krags.

They went up the shell-pocked hill with hardly a casualty. It was in the bag. The barbed wire that the Boeing-Douglas people had hurriedly strung was all but leveled by the barrage. They were within fifty feet of the ravaged enemy trenches when the shattering blast hit them.

Joe Mauser had never run into such a heavy fire.

125

Even as he fell, he saw his lads go down, to right and left, like mowed wheat.

He rolled desperately into a shallow shell hole, seeking cover. He had taken two hits, one in his side, one in his right leg. Panting, he checked them. Evidently, both were of small caliber. If they had been Maxim, not to speak of Gatling gun slugs, he would have had it. He fumbled for his first aid kit.

So the infallible Stonewall Cogswell wasn't as infallible as all that, he thought bitterly. Whether or not the International Disarmament Commission voted against them later, enforcing the Universal Disarmament Pact, Bitter Dave Langenscheidts's lads had their *mitrailleuse* and a hell of a lot of them.

He didn't dare raise his head to check out what had come of his lads. For a moment, the deadly fire dropped off. Probably, the marksmen had emptied their pans of ammo, he decided, and were reloading. And it was then that Jim Hawkins, bent double to make as small a target as possible, appeared at the edge of the shell hole.

"Joe!" he yelped. "Are you all right? As soon as I saw you fall, I came a-running."

"Get down!" Joe yelled.

But it was then that the blast of automatic fire hit Jim Hawkins, cutting him nearly in two.

At that point Joe Mauser awoke from his nightmare. There were blisters of sweat on his forehead and running rivulets of perspiration all over his body. He lay there in his bed for long minutes, panting.

Joe remembered how the rest of the fracas had been a madhouse. Stonewall Cogswell had taken a devastating blow, but had not been eliminated. In that frontal assault he had lost practically all of his infantry field officers. Joe had been field-promoted to acting battalion commander, then to acting regimental commander, and finally to acting brigadier. For three days he held the rank of acting commander of brigade.

It had finally ended when Jack Altshuler's heavy cavalry hit Bitter Dave Langenscheidt from the rear, decisively overrunning him. Joe, when it was over, was bounced from High-Lower to Low-Middle at the same time as he acquired Rank First Lieutenant. His victory, however, was cotton in his mouth. Jim Hawkins had copped his last one on the way to Joe's rescue, a rescue that wasn't necessary.

He stumbled out of his bed and made his way to the bathroom. It had been the last time that Joe Mauser had ever done any drinking immediately before or during a fracas. If Jim hadn't been drenched, old pro that he was, he would never have run into that sheet of fire while coming to Joe's aid. He might have crawled on his belly, from shell hole to shell hole, but he would never have come running erect.

Joe showered in cold water, used a depilatory on his beard, then returned to the bedroom and dressed. He was still shaken. His dreams and particularly his nightmares were more than ordinarily vivid and believable. He wished that Nadine was available to give him a lift, but she had taken a trip to the West Coast, somewhat similar to the one that had taken him to Mexico City, to contact a group out there.

He went on into the living room and through it to the small dining room with its auto-chef table. He dialed black coffee and returned with it to the living room where he found Max Mainz with a handful of leaflets and pamphlets and a pleased grin on his face.

Joe said, "Morning, Max. Did you go to the Nathan Hale Society rally?"

"Sure," Max said. He handed over the Society literature. "It wasn't as big as all that. Maybe two or

127

three hundred cloddies. And most of them probably wouldn'ta come if it hadn't been for free beer and trank."

Joe sat on the couch and looked at the material Max had brought. He said, "How would the crowd break down caste-wise?"

"Almost all of them were Lowers," Max told him. "And Low-Lowers at that."

Joe looked up. "No Middles? No Uppers?"

"I dint see more than maybe half a dozen Middles and they dint look like they come to cheer. Just maybe kind of curious. One kinda heckled the first speaker and a couple of the guards beat him up. There was a special place for the Uppers to sit and they had champagne and all. There was maybe twenty-five or thirty of them, but I don't know if they was members or just possible recruits. All the speakers looked like Uppers."

Joe went back to the pamphlets. They were expensively printed and well done. The cover of the first one read, *My Country Right or Wrong,* and there was a depiction of Nathan Hale, his arms tied behind him, a handkerchief tied over his eyes, about to be shot as the spy he had been.

Joe muttered, "I thought it was Stephen Decatur who said that, not Nathan Hale."

He read the first few paragraphs. They seemed to have been written for the eyes of a twelve-year-old and not a very bright one at that.

Max sat down and said, "I joined up."

Joe looked at him, startled. "You what?"

"I joined up. I'm going to be a Minuteman. You get to wear a special blue shirt and you carry a billy club around and beat up anybody who gives the Society a hard time."

Joe glared at him. "You damned cloddy."

"Well, Zen, Major, you told me to learn as much

about them as I could. So now I'm right in with them. I'll get the inside dope. Besides, they're not so bad. Patriotic, like. There's just one thing that worries me."

"What's that?" Now that he thought about it, having a plant in the ranks of the Nathan Hale Society might not be a bad idea.

Max said, scowling, "Well, when I signed up it was with Baron Balt Haer. And he said that they'd check out my Category Security dossier. If it checked out okay, then I'd be a full member."

"Holy Jumping Zen, Max. If they find out that you're associated with me, you'll wind up dead. Nobody's supposed to have access to your Security dossier except proper government officials."

"Yeah," Max said, "By the looks of it, the Society and Category Security are, like, buddy-buddy. One of the big Security officials was the first speaker last night. I betcha he's a member of the Society."

Joe mulled it over. He said, "There's a half dozen things in your dossier that would connect you to me. You were my batman in two fracases. You were my observer the first time I used a glider. You went with me to Budapest on that mission to contact the Sov-world underground. And right now you're paying part of the rent on this apartment."

"Yeah," Max said miserably. "Baron Haer's already got my signature and my identification number."

Joe hurried over to the table and to the telly-phone there. He dialed the special unlisted number Frank Hodgson had given him and drew a blank. Seemingly, the bureaucrat was neither in his office nor his home.

Joe dialed Philip Holland on *his* unlisted, organizational phone, and this time the other's face faded in.

Joe Mauser said quickly, "Emergency. Max joined up with Balt's outfit last night, and Balt dropped the information that they'd check out his Security dossier.

Is there any possible manner in which to remove any information connecting Max to me?"

"Will do, soonest," Holland snapped. "Get him out of your apartment and into another one. Not a fancy one. He's only a Middle-Lower. Maybe this isn't too bad an idea, Joe, having a man planted in with those funkers."

Philip Holland's face faded.

Joe spun back to Max Mainz. "Get your things packed, Max. We don't know whether or not we can get to that dossier before Baron Haer checks it. He already suspects me as being anti-government, and if he finds out any connection between us, your name's mud."

"You're the boss, Joe." Max looked around the room. "Gee, I really liked living in this place. It's going to be tough, going back to Lower quarters."

Chapter Thirteen

Max Mainz was taken aback by the magnitude of the Headquarters of the Nathan Hale Society when he approached it Saturday night. Several days had passed since some contact of Joe's had erased from Max's Security dossier the pertinent information linking him to Joe Mauser. He and Joe had kept their fingers crossed in the meantime, but nothing had developed that would indicate that the Society had checked on Max before Joe's friend had taken action.

He assumed that he would soon know, one way or the other. He was entering the lion's den. He wasn't too unhappy. According to Joe Mauser, some big mucky-muck in Joe's organization, whoever it was—Max didn't know the name of anybody else who belonged, except Nadine Haer—had promised to pay Max well if he came up with any useable information.

He entered the main doorway, passing two king-size Minutemen who were standing there, billy clubs in sheaths at their sides.

Max approached the nearest, a stupid looking oaf, and almost certainly a Low-Lower. His cheap clothing indicated that.

Max said, "I'm a new member. This is the first time I ever been here. Where do I go?"

The other grinned at him. "Right on through and straight on back. They got a big party going on. Bunch of chorus girls and all. Damn it. I hafta pull guard duty tonight."

Max entered into a large lobby where there were several reception desks, though at this time of the evening they were unoccupied.

He looked around, highly impressed. Admittedly,

this was the national as well as the local headquarters; nevertheless, it gave a clue to the resources of the Nathan Hale Society. Max whistled silently. He could hear the sounds of the party toward the rear of the building and made his way in that direction. An orchestra was blasting away, doing its best to make itself heard above the clamor.

When Max had pushed his way through the swinging doors, he stopped for a moment and stared. The room was done in the decor of the Old West, an ultra-large saloon-cum-nightclub. An old-fashioned bar ran the full length of one side of the room parallel to a line of booths on the other. Live bartenders, a rarity these times, though not unknown even in the days of auto-bars, were busily supplying the needs of about a hundred men, most of them in Minutemen shirts. There were large numbers of others seated in the booths and at tables scattered around the center of the saloon. Waiters scurried about filling orders for these. At the far end of the room was a stage; before it, a live orchestra of six men. On the stage, eight topless girls, nearly bottomless, for that matter, were dancing with more enthusiasm than art. Half of their audience was drunkenly cheering them on.

Max headed for the bar, though it looked as though he'd have his troubles ever getting through the mass of drinkers.

To one side near the rear door stood Balt Haer, talking to a tough-looking Minuteman.

"That's the one I mentioned," Haer said.

Jerry looked over at Max. "Yeah. I met him at the rally. He says that he's Category Military, but he looks kinda small to be a sojer."

Balt Haer shook his head. "No. He's a Rank Private. I checked him out. He fought under me once, when I was still in the Category Military. I don't truly remember him, but his dossier says he was in one of the fracases my corporation fought. He looks wiry and aggressive, and that small build gives him a certain amount of camouflage. Nobody would take him for a tough."

Baron Haer continued to consider Max, who was across the room. Then he said, "See that he has a good time, Jerry. After the show, see that he gets first pick of the girls and see that he gets laid. Then bring him to my office."

"Yes, sir," Jerry said as he turned and headed in the direction of Max Mainz.

Max wasn't having much luck in getting himself a position at the bar. The place was packed. Ordinarily, in spite of his size, or possibly because of it, Max was well on the feisty side. But this was his first appearance at the Society's headquarters, and he had no desire to get into trouble. Besides, he had arrived late, and most of these cloddies were already at least half drenched. It would seem that the Nathan Hale Society spared no expense in the entertainment of its storm troopers.

Somebody came up beside him and said in feigned pleasure. "Max!"

Max didn't recognize him at first but then did. "Oh, hi, Jerry. I just got here. Baron Haer told me to turn up tonight to finish off my application for membership."

Jerry put an arm around the smaller man's shoulders. "Great," he gushed. "But there's no hurry. I'll see you get processed okay. First, let's have some drinks and a few laughs."

He nudged a couple of Minutemen at the end of the bar and said, with authority, "Come on, you cloddies, make room. The Baron wants this new member to have a good time."

They grudgingly made sufficient room for Max and Jerry to get their elbows onto the bar. Jerry made a commanding motion to one of the bartenders, who hurried down to them. Evidently, Max decided, this Jerry funker had a certain amount of rank among the Minutemen and in the Society in general. He had been on the committee at the rally, and now he was giving with orders.

Jerry said to Max, "Bourbon highball?"

"Zen, yes. Usually I can't afford nothing but pseudo-whiskey or beer."

Jerry said to the bartender, "Two double bourbon highballs. My chum-pal, here, has got a lot of catching up to do. I want you should give him plenty of service the rest of the night."

"Yes, sir," the other said respectfully and hurried off for bourbon bottle and ginger ale.

It was the first time Max Mainz had ever heard a Lower addressed as "Sir." He was impressed. Maybe this Nathan Hale Society wasn't such a bad deal at that. He looked down to the stage, where the semi-nude chorus girls were prancing.

"Zen," he said. "Look at the ass on that little platinum blonde."

"It's all yours," Jerry said expansively.

The drinks were shoved in front of them.

"How do you mean?" Max said.

"I mean they all put out. This is your first Society party, so you can have firsts with her, before she gets all worn down. You know, nobody wants seconds. Or tenths. Some of these cloddies are real slobs. Before the girls get to go home, they're walking bowlegged."

Max took a deep pull at his drink, impressed. He looked back at the high kicking little platinum blonde.

"Zen," he said. "She don't look like no mopsy."

"We get the best," Jerry said. "Nobody wants to screw a beast. Only the best."

Max took another pull at his drink, which he thought was more than a double, and maybe a triple. On top of

134

that, it was good bourbon. Max had had precious little whiskey in his life and practically no really genuine whiskey. A Lower didn't drink much good liquor these days.

Jerry told him, "Some of the biggest men in the country are members of the Society. They don't mind none about shelling out. They can afford it. And Minutemen don't get paid nothing, ordinarily. It's a volunteer organization, like. Patriotic, see? So the Society throws these little bashes for them."

Max looked about the room. "No women members, eh?"

"Hell, no. We don't hold with women being in politics and things like that. We don't even think they oughta be able to vote. It's unladylike. We also don't believe niggers and kikes ought to vote."

"Yeah, sure," Max said. His eyes went back to the stage. "Man, that's some ass," he said. To his surprise, his glass was empty.

Jerry ordered another for him. His own drink was still only partially touched.

After the drink had come and Max had taken a preliminary sip, Jerry said, "This is the life, Max. You can't beat it when you're only a Lower. Who the hell could afford this sort of living it up on the dividends a Lower gets from his Inalienable Basic?"

"Yeah," Max said.

The chorus girls had wound up their dance and were prancing from the stage to thundrous applause and shouts.

Jerry smirked and said, "See that door over next to where the orchestra is? Go on through there. Maybell will be in Room Three. I'll see you later. The Baron wants to talk to you."

Max gulped his drink. "Yeah, sure," he said. "You sure it's all set up? What'll it cost me?"

Jerry simulated indignation. "Zen, you're a Minute-man, Max. It's all on the house." He grinned lewdly. "Just don't wear her down to the point where there's nothing left for nobody else."

"These here girls clean?" Max said.

"Clean? Hell we have 'em all examined by a doc just before they come in here."

"I don't like to take no chances," Max said. "I never had a dose of clap in my life."

He took off. Max was surprised at the potency of the drinks. Hell, they weren't just triples; they were quadruples. He wondered why in the hell Joe Mauser was against these people.

Finding Room Three was no problem. Max knocked politely and a voice said, "It's open, dear."

Max went in. Maybell was there. She was still topless and now she was barefoot; she'd been dancing all evening and her feet were killing her. But she was able to come up with a welcoming smile. Closer up, she looked a bit more aged than she had been on the stage, but she was still pushing one hundred percent in womanhood, so far as Max was concerned.

She grinned at him mischievously and said, in a husky voice, "I know what you got in mind."

Max went over and pushed her back onto the bed. He pulled off her rompers which were sweaty from her dancing and slightly stained. It didn't seem to make much difference, either to him or to her. Jerry had been right. By Max's standards this was pretty high-quality merchandise. And it was all for free. Hell, he hadn't even bought her a drink.

She gasped, "Zen!" and then, "Don't you even want to kiss me a little?"

"No," he said. "Spread your legs." Max had never kissed a whore in his life and he wasn't about to begin now.

136

It was all over in a brutally short time. Without looking back at her, or speaking to her again, Max went into the bathroom and cleaned himself up. He had heard somewhere that if you washed immediately after laying a mopsy you ran little chance of VD. Jerry had assured him that all of the girls had been medically inspected and he assumed that it was true. And he'd been the first to take this one, so he was comparatively safe. He grunted cynically and wondered what shape these girls would be in by the time the evening was over.

He returned to the hall and then to the party. There was already a line out in front of the bedroom door from which he had emerged.

Jerry, his face leering, was awaiting him. "You get fixed up with Maybell?" he said.

"Yeah," Max said.

"How was she? I never sampled it. Never got around to it. I kinda like that redhead when this here crew comes on "

Max Mainz made a rocking motion with his hand. "Not bad. I guess she was a little tired from the dancing."

Jerry scowled. "I know what you mean. No bounce in her fanny, eh? I think maybe I'll recommend to the entertainment committee that we have two sets of girls. Some for the entertaining out here and another gang back there for the screwing. And we oughta get more girls in the back rooms. They get kinda oily after awhile, you know what I mean. You want another drink, Max?"

"Maybe later. Maybe I oughta see the Baron. You said he wanted to see me."

"Okay, come on."

Jerry led the way through a door and to an elevator

bank. Max was impressed. These headquarters of the Nathan Hale Society were really swank.

As they took the elevator to higher levels, Max said, "How come you call it the Nathan Hale Society?"

Jerry looked blank. "Damned if I know. The outfit's run by Uppers. Some, kinda like eggheads. They dreamed up the name. Here we are."

The elevator came to a halt. There were two Minutemen stationed at either side, armed with billy clubs. They looked at Max suspiciously but obviously knew Jerry and waved them on.

Jerry led the way down the hall and to a door flanked by two more Minutemen. Letters in gold on the door proclaimed *Baron Balt Haer Commander-in-Chief*.

One of the Minutemen said, "Hi, Jerry."

Jerry said, "We got an appointment with the Baron."

"Just a minute, Jerry," the Minuteman said, and disappeared behind the door.

When he returned, it was to say, "Okay."

They went through a reception room dominated by one desk, behind which sat a Category Military of Rank Colonel.

He looked up from his paperwork and said, "My country, may she always be right..."

And Jerry said, "But my country, right or wrong."

The Colonel said, "The Baron is awaiting you."

Jerry knew the way. He opened a door to the Colonel's left and allowed Max to precede him.

Balt Haer sat importantly behind the desk.

He said, "Ah, Max Mainz, isn't it?" He democratically held out a hand for a shake.

Max leaned over the desk and shook the other's hand, although Haer hadn't bothered to come to his feet. Max hadn't expected him to. In fact, he was surprised at the offer of a handshake. Baron Haer, after all, was a Mid-Upper and Max was a Mid-Lower.

"Sit down, sit down," Balt Haer said. "I checked out your dossier, Max. Born a Low-Lower, Category Food, Subdivision Cooking, Branch Chef. Obviously, a category that has all but completely been automated out of existence. So, being ambitious, you switched to Category Military, having had your basic training as a young man. You have thus far participated in two fracases, one under my father and one under Marshal Stonewall Cogswell. Both times you were on the winning side and received your bonus. I assume you must have distinguished yourself since you were bounced in caste to Mid-Lower. However, I am surprised that you remain a Rank Private."

"Yes, sir," Max said modestly. He wondered to what extent his dossier had been altered by whatever higher-up Joe had contacted. Max had been Joe's batman in both fracases. He hadn't had a shot fired at him. Balt Haer sounded as though Max had been an infantryman, in and out of the dill a half dozen times in the two frays. He added, "I guess they figured a bounce in caste was enough."

Balt Haer pretended indignation. "Only Rank Private? A man with your experience? I am no longer in Category Military myself. Through the foolery of a funker named Mauser, who was serving under me at the time, I was expelled. However, I have friends. I'll utilize my connections to have you raised to Rank Sergeant. That is, if our association proves fruitful."

Max was inwardly surprised. In actuality, he hadn't planned on ever participating in a fracas again. He had associated enough with Joe Mauser to have learned that the end product of that was copping the final one.

He said, "Well, thanks, sir. But whatda'ya mean by fruitful?"

The Baron leaned back, expansively. "Max," he said, "we need more men who have seen combat. As possibly

Jerry, here, has mentioned to you, we have special squads of Minutemen who perform special tasks of an emergency sort. Ordinarily, the Minutemen are not paid by the Society. They serve out of pure patriotism. However, these special squads sometimes are called upon to render special service; whenever they do so, at least one share of Variable Basic is added to their portfolio."

Max didn't know what a portfolio was, but he looked impressed. "That sounds good," he said.

The Baron went on. "Jerry leads one of our special squads, and I propose that you join it. Right at this time we are somewhat short of good men. Recently, five of our best were lost in an operation down in Mexico, so we are short handed. What do you think, Max?"

"It sounds good to me, sir."

"Fine." The other rubbed his hands together. "We have your address, and Jerry will contact you the next time an assignment comes up. And now, why don't you two go on back to the party and bend a few elbows?"

It was a dismissal. Jerry and Max got up, made their formal farewells, and left.

Max didn't have the vaguest idea of what the Baron's special squads ordinarily did, but he realized that those five who had jumped Joe and him in Mexico must have made up one of them.

Chapter Fourteen

Max and Jerry returned to the saloon and made their way back to their former position at the bar's end. The place wasn't quite so packed now.

Jerry grinned knowingly and said, "Some of 'em are back in the hall lined up in front of the doors of the girls' rooms. Those mopsies are going to be a weary lot before morning. Some of the guys knock off a piece with one, then go back and get in line for another one. Art Prager claims he once laid all eight, but he's a goddamned liar."

The nearest bartender had recognized them and came down with two more bourbon highballs.

Max Mainz took his and looked around the room. At least a dozen of the Minutemen were already passed out at tables or booths. A waiter was mopping up where one had vomited.

He came back to Jerry and said, "These assignments your special squad gets. What for instance?"

"Aw, usually not much. One time we went out and beat up some school kids who were demonstrating against something or other. Another time we went and lit fire to a kike synagogue. Imagine a synagogue in Greater Washington. Why can't these bastards join the Category Religion Temple, like everybody else?"

"Yeah," Max said. "But what was that the Baron said about losing five guys in an operation in Mexico? That sounds like it's tougher than beating up a bunch of students."

Jerry looked evasive. "I don't know about that one, he told Max. "Probably just a bunch of greasers. I don't know why the govmint ever let Mexico into the United States of the Americas."

Max didn't see Freddy Soligen enter the room. The newcomer stood at the door, much as Max had done earlier, and looked about. It was obviously the first time he had been here. He spotted Max at the bar and frowned, as though trying to place him, but then shook his head.

He approached one of the tables. "How do I find Baron Haer?"

One of the Minutemen pointed and said, "Through that door and down the hall aways is an elevator. The Baron's office is on the sixth floor. You'll have shit's own time gettin' in to see him unless you got an appointment."

"Thanks."

He ran into no interference until he reached the sixth floor and found two guards there, armed with billy clubs. They gave him the cold eye, then moved in on him and gave him a quick but thorough frisking. Freddy Soligen bore it stoically.

One of them said, "What the hell do you want?"

Freddy said, "To see Baron Haer."

"You got an appointment?" the other guard said.

"No, but I think he'll see me."

"Whatda'ya want to see him about?"

Whatever else Freddy Soligen was, he was no coward. He looked the other straight in the eye and said, "That's none of your business, chum-pal."

The two glared at him. One finally said, "Go down the hall there until you see an office with two more Minutemen there."

"What's a Minuteman?"

The guard tapped the snake on his shirt and said pompously, "We wear shirts like this."

That didn't seem to exactly answer the question, but Freddy shrugged it off and headed down the hall as indicated.

He had no difficulty locating the guarded office. He said to one of the two Minutemen, "I'd like to see Baron Haer."

"Got an appointment, friend?"

"No, but I think he'll see me. My name is Freddy Soligen."

"The Fracas News telly reporter?" the younger of the two asked.

"That's right," Freddy sighed.

"Zen! I seen you a dozen times. Sometimes one of the other cameramen would get you in lens. Always right in the middle of the dill. I'll never forget that time when Union Carbide was having it out with Monsanto and . . ."

"I won't forget it either," Freddy sighed. "I copped one. Now how do I go about seeing the Baron?"

The Minuteman frowned. "I'll go in and ask Colonel Buttrick."

He went through the door and while he was gone the older Minuteman frisked Freddy again. "Just routine," he said, slightly apologetically.

"It's okay," Freddy said. "I never packed a shooter in my life."

The younger one came back and said, "Colonel Buttrick will see you, Citizen Soligen."

Freddy could have asked who the hell Colonel Buttrick was, but didn't bother. He went through the door the Minuteman held open for him. A typical fracas-buff, Freddy thought. He could take his shirt off without unbuttoning his collar. It was for the likes of him that Freddy had risked his butt a hundred times over.

The moment he saw Colonel Buttrick, sitting behind the receptionist's desk, Freddy Soligen recognized him. He'd covered several fracases the colonel had participated in.

He said, "Hi, Colonel, it's been a long time. You were in the dill on that New Mexico Military Reservation. The United Miners, American Federation of Labor fracas. You were commanding the United Miners' light cavalry."

The colonel stood up, smiled, and extended a hand. "Yes, I recall it very well. You gave me excellent coverage, Freddy. It was largely through you that I received my full colonel's rank in the Category Military."

Freddy shook and said, "What's the chances of me seeing the Baron?"

"Could you tell me why? He's always frightfully busy. He carries the full load of the burden of the Nathan Hale Society."

From what Freddy Soligen knew of Balt Haer, it couldn't have been much of a burden if the Baron was carrying it.

He said, "I'm afraid not. It's sort of a top-secret thing—pertaining to your Society, and for his ears only."

The other nodded, frowning only slightly. "I've already notified the Baron of your request for an interview."

An interview wasn't exactly what Freddy had in him, but he held his peace.

Something on the colonel's desk buzzed, and he flicked a switch, listened for a moment, and then looked at Freddy and said, "The Baron can give you five minutes."

Freddy Soligen suspected that he needed a sight more than five minutes, but he let the future take care of that. A door opened automatically next to Colonel Buttrick, and Freddy marched through into the opulent office that Max Mainz had occupied less than an hour before. Balt Haer, looking important, was seated behind the desk.

He said, "Hello, Citizen Soligen. I admit that my association with you wasn't under the most happy of circumstances, but I assume that was not your fault. You were merely doing your job." He hadn't offered to shake hands, but Freddy took the chair he indicated.

Freddy Soligen said, "Yes, sir. I was in that glider with my telly camera the second time Joe Mauser flew it in a fracas. It led to both you and him being kicked out of the Category Military for violating the Universal Disarmament Pact. I had to testify at the court martial afterward, but it had nothing to do with me."

"No. Of course not. And now, what is the purpose of your visit, Citizen Soligen? The Nathan Hale Society is always most cooperative with the Category Communications, but your particular field is Branch Fracas News, and we hardly come under that."

Freddy said, "No. Let me give you some background, sir. I was born a Lower. I'm ambitious. Doing it the hard way, I worked my way up to Low-Middle. Which still isn't very high in this People's Capitalism of ours. I repeat, I'm ambitious."

Balt Haer said impatiently, "I don't see how that applies to either the Society or myself, Soligen."

"No, sir. However, I know that your old man, uh, that is your father, Baron Haer, had quite a bit of influence in the Department of Categories. I don't know how much of this has come down to you."

"I see," Balt Haer said coldly. "You would like me to utilize what influence I can to have you bounced in your caste."

"Yes, sir."

"And what do you offer in return, assuming I could make such arrangements?"

Freddy Soligen took a deep breath before speaking. He said, "Baron Haer, I was recently contacted by someone who offered to raise my rank in Category Communications to Rank Commentator. It's the highest rank in my category, sir. News Commentators are usually Upper-Middles or even Uppers. The pay is good."

Balt Haer knew the other was a top fracas telly reporter, but he did not seem to be of News Commentator caliber. He said, "Who offered you this promotion?"

"The man we were talking about earlier. Joe Mauser."

The baron stared at him. "Joe Mauser is in no position to honor that committment."

"He isn't?"

"He is suspected of being a subversive and is being investigated by the Nathan Hale Society."

"I see."

"You're a friend of his?" Balt Haer asked suspiciously.

"I'm even more so a friend of mine—and of my son. I want him to be in line for a bounce or two in caste, as well as myself. He's an adult now, so any bounce I get doesn't automatically reflect on his caste."

"Just a minute," Balt Haer said. He flicked on his desk screen and said, "Buttrick, see if Colonels Fodor and Warren are working late tonight. If they are, give them my compliments and ask them to come to my office."

He flicked the set off and turned back to Freddy and said, "I told you that Mauser is suspected of being a subversive."

"It's no suspicion, Baron. He is. He told me so himself when he offered me the job."

"Why did he offer it to you—assuming he could deliver it?"

"I'm not too clear. I think his organization wants to infiltrate Category Communications. You can see how it is. They'll need men in key news spots when they try to pull whatever it is they want to pull."

"Very well, what is it you are offering and what are you asking?"

"A bounce or two in caste and the same for my son."

"And what do you give in return?"

"Like you said, Joe Mauser doesn't have the pull to make me a Rank Commentator. That mean's there's somebody else in his outfit with enough pull who can do it."

Balt Haer viewed him skeptically. "It would take a rather high government official to be able to pull such strings; not necessarily someone in Category Communications; but someone who had close contacts with them."

"Yes, sir," Freddy said, feeling he was beginning to get across now. "And how was Joe bounced up to Upper caste? He had only been a Mid-Middle; then, right after his court martial, he was bounced two castes. That doesn't make much sense. He was lucky they didn't reduce him a couple of castes."

Baron Haer looked at him for a long moment. He said finally, "What you're saying is that the government has been infiltrated by subversives on a very high level."

And Freddy Soligen looked back. "What's it worth to you to find out who they are, Baron?"

But it was then that the door opened and two in the uniform of Category Military, Rank Lieutenant-Colonel entered.

Balt Haer began introductions, but the newcomers anticipated him. Both advanced on Freddy Soligen with extended hands.

Lieutenant-Colonel Michael Fodor said, "Why, Freddy, I haven't seen you since that interview during the fracas in Louisiana." There was only slight condescension in his voice; after all, he was an Upper addressing a Middle and in a quite friendly manner.

"No, sir," Freddy said. "You put on a good show there, Colonel."

Paul Warren was more open. He smiled as he shook and said, "I'll never forget the time you were covering Stonewall Cogswell when he got that shock of seeing Joe Mauser's glider up there observing him right smack in the middle of a fracas."

Freddy grinned in reply. "He sure was shocked all right."

Balt Haer said stiffly, "Gentlemen and Citizen Soligen, shall we get down to business?"

When all were seated, the Baron gave a resume of what Freddy Soligen had told him.

Lieutenant-Colonel Paul Warren scowled unhappily and said, "Joe Mauser?"

And Balt Haer said, "I never did trust him, and now he's obviously up to his ears in a subversive movement. Our duty, as officers of the Nathan Hale Society, is to expose him and particularly these high-ranking government officials that he seems to front for." He turned his eyes to Freddy Soligen and said, "I do not wield the influence that my late father did. However, the Society has high connections. I guarantee that if you can reveal to us the traitors you mention, you will be bounced in caste to Upper-Middle and your son..."

"Sam," Freddy said.

"Yes, your son, Sam, as well. What category is he in?"

"Category Military."

"Yes, then we shall see that he is promoted in rank, as well."

Paul Warren took exception. "Joe Mauser was always a good man," he said. "I've been in more than one fracas with him. He once saved my life."

Freddy looked at him and nodded. "Yeah. You were usually on Stonewall Cogswell's permanent staff, and

148

sometimes Mauser was with him. How come you've not up with the Marshal on the Little Big Horn Military Reservation? He's going into another fracas with old Bitter Dave Langenscheidt. This will be the fifth fracas those two have fought. I'm surprised they don't have it out with pitchforks one of these days."

Warren said, "It's only regimental magnitude. The former marshal is only a brigadier these days but he's drastically cut back his staff. I'm no longer on it."

Baron Haer said impatiently, "This is all beside the point, gentlemen and Citizen Soligen. The point is that the former Major Mauser is a traitor to People's Capitalism and the Ultra-Welfare State. He and his criminal associates must be exposed."

Freddy stood and said, "All right, so it's a deal. I find out who the government officials are who are able to bounce Joe up two castes and who are able to up my rank in Category Communications to News Commentator. In return, you bounce me and my son."

Balt Haer nodded. "You have my word."

Freddy Soligen turned to go, but then cocked his head in thought. He snapped his fingers and said, "Talking about Joe Mauser and Stonewall Cogswell just brought something to mind."

Baron Haer viewed him impatiently. He wanted to get rid of the telly reporter and talk the whole thing over with Michael Fodor and Paul Warren. "What?" he said.

"I just saw Max Mainz in the nightclub. At first, I didn't recognize him. But now it comes back to me."

"Who in the hell's Max Mainz?" Fodor said. "And what difference does it make?"

Freddy said, "He used to be Joe Mauser's batman. Back in that fracas when he first flew the glider, Mainz was his observer, or signalman. The second time Joe used the glider, the time they nailed him, I took over so I could cover it for telly and Max was pissed off, jealous.

149

That's when I met him—at the airport. Only briefly, but it was him, all right. Come to think of it, I've seen him with Joe on another occasion. When Joe Mauser fought that Sov-officer in the duel in Budapest, it was televised, and at one time I spotted Mainz, along with other embassy Americans, in the background."

"Max Mainz," Paul Warren said. "It comes back to me. It was election day in Kingston on the outskirts of the Catskill Military Reservation. Election day, when all castes can mix. Lowers can go into Upper bars, restaurants, and even hotels. Joe Mauser, a captain then, came into the Upper bar there with his orderly. You were there, Balt, and so was the Sov-world colonel, Lajos Arpad, or whatever his name was, who was connected with the International Disarmament Commission as an observer to see that the Universal Disarmament Pact was being observed."

Balt Haer was looking shocked. He said, "Now that you mention it, I do remember. That's where I've seen the man before. That clod, Mauser, had the gall to introduce him."

"Yes, Max Mainz was the name all right," Warren nodded.

Freddy Soligen said, "What in the name of Holy Jumping Zen's he doing down there with your Minutemen, or whatever you call them?"

Balt Haer's lips had gone pale. He said, "Let me think for a minute. Yesterday, I read his Category Security dossier. There was nothing in it that mentioned that he had been Joe Mauser's orderly. And certainly nothing in it that mentioned that he had accompanied Mauser to Budapest. How in the world could that be? It would *have* to be in his dossier. *Everything* is in a man's Security dossier."

Michael Fodor said softly, "It means that these officials that bounced Mauser to Low-Upper and have offered Freddy, here, a rise in rank to Commentator are even higher placed than we suspected. It means that they're in position to alter Category Security dossiers."

"That's practically impossible," Warren blurted.

Fodor looked at him.

Balt Haer ran the back of his right hand over his mouth. He said, very slowly, "I've often wondered why the information I've submitted to Category Security about my sister's hairbrained flirtations with subversives never turned up on her dossier."

Freddy said, "Well, this is all your problem, not mine. All I know is, Max Mainz is down in your saloon getting drenched with your Minutemen. And now, we've made a deal. Good night."

He turned and left.

Balt Haer looked from one to the other of his two fellow officers of the Nathan Hale Society. He said, "The man just joined up. He's obviously a goddamned spy. Gentlemen, I think we've just been given another tool which will enable us to completely repudiate this mysterious subversive organization."

Chapter Fifteen

After Joe Mauser finished breakfast, the telly-phone buzzed and when he answered it, Nadine Haer's face faded in.

She smiled her love-smile for him and said, "Hello, darling. I'm back."

"Mission accomplished?"

"Well, no."

"What happened?"

"I shouldn't discuss it over the phone. H and H are coming over to my place to work it around. We'll also have an opportunity to go over our interview with the doctor the other day. Can you come soonest? Their time is limited, of course."

"I'll be there, sweetie."

She looked at him mockingly. "Sweetie?" she said. "You sound like a teenager."

"I feel like one when I see you."

"I'll discuss that further with you tonight."

"It's a date." Her face faded from the telly screen.

Then the identity screen on the door rang. The face there was that of Freddy Soligen. Joe activated the door and went into the living room, an extra coffee cup in hand.

He said, "Hi, chum-pal."

The friendly salutation set Freddy back, but wordlessly he took the proffered coffee and sank down into a chair. Joe took the couch.

Freddy said, "Joe, I've been having second thoughts."

"Oh, such as what?"

"My protection. The deal you offered me the other day; it has angles."

"You get to be a Rank Commentator," Joe said.

"So you say, but you're messing around with a very hot fire, Joe. What happens if a wheel comes off? You're dealing with the Bureau of Investigation, the Category Security, and such amateur outfits as the Nathan Hale Society. Any of them can be tough."

"We have good cover for our people, Freddy. We're not a bunch of mollies."

"So you say, so you say. But you're talking about overthrowing the government, and you're putting me in a position so that I can help. I told you how I stood the other day. Sure, I'd like a Rank Commentator deal. But how do I know, even if you can swing it, that I wouldn't wind up booted out of Category Communications altogether, like you were booted out of Category Military—and maybe with a slammer sentence on top of that?"

"Our cover is really tops, Freddy," Joe said, finishing his coffee.

"Who?" Freddy said flatly.

"That's top secret," Joe said reasonably. "Take my word for it. I'm going to see them this morning and tell them about you. They'll put things to work. I think that you'll be a telly Rank Commentator before the week is out."

Freddy said, "Listen, Joe, I'm not a kid. Before I stick my neck out before the Bureau of Investigation and Category Security, I want to know it's safe."

Joe Mauser made a decision. "Freddy," he said. "The head of the Bureau of Investigation *is* one of your covers."

Freddy Soligen gaped at him. "You're drivel-happy, Joe. The head of the Bureau of Investigation is Wallace Pepper. He's a drunken bum."

"Don't be naive," Joe sighed. "The real head of the North American Bureau of Investigation is Frank

Hodgson. He's no more than an Upper-Middle, or something like that, but he's the one who runs the Bureau. Pepper is only an Upper figurehead. The same thing applies to some of our other top members. Philip Holland, for instance, the man behind Harlow Mannerheim, supposedly our Minister of Foreign Affairs."

"You mean that you people have infiltrated that far up in the government?" Freddy said in disbelief.

"Yes," Joe told him patiently. "How do you think I got to be an Upper? That was a two-caste bounce."

Freddy Soligen made a motion of acceptance with his right hand after putting down his cup. "Okay," he said. "You swing the promotion, Joe, and I'm with you."

Joe stood to accompany him to the door. "You look a bit preoccupied, Freddy."

Freddy nodded. "Yeah," he said. "Sam has joined up with Stonewall Cogswell's side in that new fracas between him and Bitter Dave."

"Oh?" Joe looked worried. "That's not so good. I have a feeling those two will really have it out this time. Over the years that grudge between them has been getting worse and worse, not better."

"Stonewall will lick him again," Freddy said, at the door. "He's licked him four times and he'll do it again." He hesitated momentarily before adding, "But not without taking plenty of casualties. Sam's still a greenhorn as far as the fracases are concerned."

Inwardly, Joe agreed with him, but didn't want to add to the little man's worries.

When Freddy Soligen was gone, Joe went over to his transport terminal and dialed for a vacuum-tube capsule. He hoped that he wasn't holding up the meeting at Nadine's place but Freddy hadn't been with him very long. When the two-seater capsule arrived, he got in and dialed directly through to the Haer mansion.

He emerged in the living room and Nadine came

over to welcome him, her lips raised for a kiss. Joe did his best.

"Hello, darling," she said.

Frank Hodgson and Philip Holland were seated side by side on one of the couches. Both rose and shook hands.

Phil Holland said, "How'd that thing with your man Mainz and the Nathan Hale Society work out? Did I get those changes in his Security dossier worked out in time?"

"I don't know yet," Joe said worriedly. "Max was scheduled to go to their headquarters last night. If you didn't get the changes done in time, he probably got himself into the soup. Is there any way we can check?"

"Not that I know of," Holland said. "Long since, I suppose, we should have planted some of our membership in the Nathan Hale Society, but we didn't. For one thing, it's composed almost entirely of Lowers, except for those at the head. And we draw a blank when it comes to Lowers among our membership."

The three men reseated themselves.

"Coffee, anybody?" Nadine said.

"I just had coffee," Joe said, but the other two accepted and Nadine left to get it.

"A complete blank?" Joe said.

Hodgson said, disgust in his voice, "We don't have a single Low-Lower in our ranks. We have a few Upper-Lowers, largely men and women who should be Middles, but have been passed over by the Department of Categories when it came to bounces. There's more and more of that, by the way. It's getting much more difficult by the month to up your caste. Phil and I can sometimes swing it, as we did in your case, but we can't stick our necks out too often, or it would become noted."

Nadine had returned with a tray of coffee things and

155

put it on the coffee table before them.

As Hodgson poured, he looked up at her and said, "How did you do with that group on the West Coast, my dear?"

Nadine shook her head in despair and sank into a chair. "I drew a blank. They were composed largely of Upper-Lowers and especially Middles. They were another group of reformists, not potential revolutionists. What they want most is an easier system of bouncing up in caste level and more Inalienable Basic shares. They'd be more likely to join the Sons of Liberty than our organization."

Frank Hodgson looked over at Joe. "It was the same with the Sons of Liberty?"

"Yes," Joe told him "It's evidently composed almost entirely of Middles who want to reform Peoples Capitalism, not overthrow it. They give lip-service to wanting to better the condition of the Lowers as well, but in actuality they're ambitious Middles wanting to make Upper."

Holland said in disgust, "It's the same old story. The slob element, the Low-Lowers, join the Nathan Hale Society and sing the praises of the Ultra-Welfare State, mainly for the free booze and the opportunity to sadistically club anybody over the head who disagrees with them. The Middles, when they join anything at all, go to some reform outfit in hopes of patching up a socioeconomic system that's beyond reform. So where is the recruit material? They are Uppers, approximately one percent of the population. But our program is to overthrow them. Some chance of gaining recruits!"

Joe was as depressed as the others at the defeatest atmosphere. He said, "Somebody mentioned the other day the need for us to recruit members of the mass media. I contacted Freddy Soligen, one of the most veteran of telly reporters. In the past he was Branch

Fracas News, but he's been thinking of switching. When I propositioned him he agreed to come over to us if we get him promoted to Rank Commentator."

Holland looked over at Frank Hodgson. He said, "We ought to be able to swing that. Burke, over at Category Communications, owes me a few favors. It wouldn't hurt us at all to have a Rank Commentator planted in telly. We're not ready to use him, as yet, but there'll come a day. For that matter, once this Soligen is in with us we might make other converts in Category Communications. We could use them."

Hodgson nodded. "Why don't you see about it, Phil? If you can't twist Burke's arm, let me know. I've got some leverage in Category Communications myself."

Chapter Sixteen

After Holland and Hodgson had left, Joe Mauser spent the balance of the day, and the night, too, for that matter, with Nadine Haer. Thus Max Mainz's efforts to get in touch with him failed. Max wasn't aware that Nadine had returned to town. Hence he didn't bother to call the Haer home in his search for Joe.

Jerry, however, had gotten in touch with him in the middle of the day on the telly phone, and said that they had an assignment for that night.

"What kind of an assignment?" Max said warily.

Jerry grinned at him from the screen. "Can't tell you that over the phone, pal. It's not much, but you'll get a share of Variable. Don't wear the shirt that I issued you, but bring the other thing. We'll pick you up in front of your building at eight. Be waiting on the curb." His face faded from the screen.

Max continued to stare at the blank telly phone screen. The other thing that Jerry had issued him was a billy club of the type the Minutemen carried. The thing to do was to get in touch with Joe soonest and find out just how to handle this. He had no doubt what the "assignment" was. Somebody was scheduled for a beating.

But he had no luck in locating Joe. The only other member of Joe's organization that Max Mainz knew was Nadine Haer, and she was out of town. If he refused to go with Jerry, then his cover in the Nathan Hale Society would be blown, Joe wanted him in the Society.

He decided that perhaps Joe's telly-phone was on the blink, and left his mini-apartment and took a hovercar over to Joe's place. Joe wasn't there, though.

At the same time, Joe was worriedly trying to get in touch with Max to find out what had happened the night before at the Nathan Hale Society headquarters. When he couldn't locate Max he gave up and returned to the joys of the woman he loved. He assumed that Max would phone him sooner or later. Either at home or at the Haer mansion.

Max was on the curb in front of his apartment house when Jerry and another Minuteman drove up in a hovercar. The two were in the front seat, and Jerry was driving. Max climbed into the back. His billy club was in his belt under his jacket.

Jerry grinned at him and said, "Max Mainz, meet Art Prager. Art's one of the best in this kinda work. Art, Max is our latest recruit. Category Military, so don't let his size throw you off. He's been in the fracases."

"Glad to meetcha," Art said. He was a very rugged-looking character and Max disliked him on sight.

Max said, "Hi, Art," and then to Jerry, nonchalantly, "What's the romp tonight?"

"Oh, nothin' important. There's this here doc belongs to some subversive outfit. Call themselves the Sons of Liberty or something like that. Bunch of kikes and atheists, that sort of shit. He's some bigshot in the outfit, so we've been checking him out and me and Art, here, have got his habits down pat. He walks his dog in the park every night at about nine. Last walk of the day for the pooch."

"Dog?" Max said. "They can be trouble. You know, I shot a dog once, three times with a forty-five and it kept coming till it was down on its belly crawling. It was one of these here Dobermans." Max was lying, but he'd seen a historical war telly show once with a Doberman in it. He was taking a desperate chance of throwing them off.

Jerry laughed. "This here's a miniature Poodle and he looks maybe twelve years old. If he sunk his teeth into you, they'd most likely drop out."

"You afraid of dogs?" Art said contemptuously.

Max had to reestablish himself. He said, hotly, "You're damned right I'm afraid of dogs like Dobermans and German Police. They're tough and if you ever been up against one of them you know it. But Poodles is another thing."

"Okay," Jerry said, obviously the leader of the assignment. "We got it all staked out. He always goes by a real quiet place, giving the little pooch a chance to piss. We hit him there."

"What'da we do?" Max said, trying to keep any apprehension from his voice.

"What'dya think we do, for Zen's sake? We work him over a little and let him know he better keep out of criticising the government and associating with kikes and foreigners, or he'll really get it the next time around. Hell, he'll probably shit in his pants. He's an old duffer. Maybe fifty-five or something. Here we are."

Jerry had entered the park. Max didn't even recognize what park it was; there were parks all over Greater Washington. Jerry came to a halt in the cover of a group of trees.

Max said, still not knowing what it was possible for him to do, "Okay." Maybe he could come through with something to ease the old guy's troubles when it came to taking a beating from these goons. One thing was sure. Max wasn't going to hit the victim. He might fake doing it, if possible, but he wouldn't hit him.

Jerry led the way down a path of shale and rock to a silent glade lit softly by the moonlight. There was a tall stand of dark trees to the far side with underbrush behind them. Jerry again led the way, and they stood in the shadows. The branches of the trees were twisting against each other in the freshening winds. Max shivered.

They remained in silence for about five minutes and then Jerry said, "Here he comes. Good old Doc Mitfield, the funker."

A middle-aged man had entered the small glade. Max couldn't make him out too well in the dim light. He was carrying a leash in his hand, but the dog who frisked about his feet was free of its leash.

"Okay, boys," Jerry said and stepped out, followed by Art. Max unhappily brought up the rear.

Doctor Lawrence Mitfield looked up at their approach, frowning. He began to say something, but Jerry and Art brought forth their billies quickly and Jerry slammed the older man across the belly, driving the wind from him and caving him forward. Art stepped in and brought his club down brutally on the doctor's head. The dog started to bark in a frenzy, but Jerry kicked him, tossing the tiny animal a full ten yards off. The two Minutemen began to beat the fallen doctor unmercifully.

"Hey, you'll kill him," Max said urgently. "He's already unconscious."

"Good idea," Art snarled. And before Max could believe what he was witnessing, the other had snatched out a snub-nosed revolver from a hip pocket, lowered it, and deliberately shot their victim behind the ear.

For a moment, Jerry, as well as Max, was stupified.

"Come on, let's get the hell out of here," Jerry said. "The cops..."

But it was then that two spotlights, from different directions, zeroed-in on them. A voice yelled, "Put 'em up, you funkers! You're covered!"

By mere chance, the three ran in differing directions. Art, his gun still in hand, tried to shoot at the spotlights as he went, and a barrage of fire reached out for him.

He went down with a scream. Jerry was dashing for the path by which they had entered the glade, probably trying to make it back to the car. Whether or not he made it, Max didn't know. He himself instinctively headed for the hedges and dove into them. All about were heaps of fallen branches and scattered stacks of underbrush left by the park's clean-up crew. He zig-zagged through them and, by so doing, unknowingly threw off the aim of the police behind. He continued to hear shots and the zing of bullets through the air above him.

He emerged into a shadowed meadow, but already he was panting and could hear sounds of pursuit. Art was possibly dead and Jerry was either shot or captured by now. The police could devote full attention to him.

He came upon a thick tangle of hawthorn hedges and forced his way through them and into another glade beyond. He still didn't have the vaguest idea of where he was. So far as he knew, he had never been in this park before, and it seemed to be fairly large. He slowed down to a walk. He could no longer hear them behind him, but if they flushed him again he'd need all of his breath. He couldn't expend the balance of his strength running madly without direction. He might even be running in a circle.

He stopped, listened, and could hear the sounds of traffic and made his way in that direction. He emerged at the edge of the park and looked up and down nervously. He crossed the boulevard and then headed down a side street.

He had to think fast, and well. This was a murder romp. And he had no way of knowing if Art was dead. He might only have copped one or two small ones. And Jerry? Jerry had been heading back for the car. They probably had nabbed him alive. Furthermore, Max had no illusions about either of the two keeping mum if they were captured. They would almost certainly implicate him.

And that meant that he couldn't go home to his own mini-apartment, and couldn't use his Universal Credit Card for transportation or anything else. The moment his identification number was revealed, the computers would be alerted for him. Any attempt to use the credit card would give them the chance to get a cross on him and zero-in.

There was just one place he could go, and he agonized about that. He didn't want to subject Joe Mauser to the risk. But the only place that held any security at all for him was Joe's apartment. And Max still had his key to it.

He emerged onto a wide boulevard and at last realized what part of town he was in. Joe's apartment was miles away; he'd have to walk. Happily, because it was still early enough in the evening, there were quite a few pedestrians on the sidewalks. He wouldn't be conspicuous.

When Joe Mauser entered his apartment the following morning, he found a bedraggled Max Mainz stretched out on the living room sofa. The room he had formerly occupied was still available, but Max hadn't made it any farther than the sofa.

Joe, scowling, shook the little man. Max opened his eyes, groggily.

"Oh, hi, Joe," he said, struggling erect and wiping his mouth with his right hand. "What time is it? You heard the morning news?"

"No," Joe said. "What news? Wait a minute. I'll get you some coffee."

"We don't have time for no coffee."

Joe Mauser sat down across from him and took him in. "No? What do we have time for?"

"A screwed-up mess," Max said. "I'm on the run. Joe, I've got a murder romp hanging over me."

Joe eyed him. "Okay. Let's hear it."

Max told him all. All about his going to the Nathan Hale Society headquarters. His meeting with Jerry. His meeting with Balt Haer. His being made a member of one of the special squads. Then the following day and his being sent on his first so-called assignment. Then the details of the assignment, the murder of Mitfield, and his escape through the park.

Joe stared at him for long moments. He said, finally, "It was a set-up."

"How do you mean?" Max said.

"It was a trap. Those cops, or Bureau of Investigation, or Category Security men, or whoever they were, were staked out, waiting for you."

Max shook his head, and said negatively, "They didn't make no effort to stop shooting that Doc Mitfield or whatever his name was."

"They didn't give a damn for him, Max " Joe said. "They wanted you."

"Me? What good am I?"

"With a murder romp charge hanging over you, probably quite a bit. Maybe your Art wasn't in on it. Maybe he was. But he was probably considered expendable. He was probably ordered to use that shooter. From what you say, not even Jerry knew he was going to do it. Art was probably a Low-Lower from what you say. It was probably set up so that you were to take the murder romp charge. Then the evidence would come out that you were connected to me. And then the evidence would come out that I was connected with the organization Nadine and I belong to. That would get both me and the organization. I smell Balt Haer's finger in the stew. When you were talking with him did he give any indication he knew you were with me?"

164

"No, and I don't think he had any such idea, Joe. He was real friendly."

Joe worked it over some more. He said finally, "While you were there, at their headquarters, before or after you saw Haer, did you run into anybody who might have been able to connect you to me?"

Max shook his head. "No. They was all these here Minutemen. Real cloddies. All Lower-Lowers and..." He paused.

"And what?"

"Come to think of it, Joe. I saw Freddy Soligen there."

"Freddy Soligen!"

"Yeah, you know, the telly reporter."

Joe Mauser's face fell. "Yes, I remember Freddy. Under what circumstances did you see him? And did he see you?"

"I don't think so. I was kind of drenched. They pass out free drinks at these here Minutemen parties. Damn good drinks. I saw him come out of the hall where you go for the elevator up to the Baron's office." —

"Holy Jumping Zen," Joe groaned. "I've screwed it up. Come on, Max, we've got some things to repair."

"Joe, I'm out like a light. I been walking and running all night. Why can't I go to bed?"

"Because, most likely, I need you. Come on." Joe Mauser went over to a drawer, opened it, brought forth his shoulder rig and his .44 Smith & Wesson, and checked the load. He took off his jacket, donned the rig, flicked the gun into it, put back on his jacket, fished a box of cartridges out, dumped them into a side pocket and turned back to Max, who was now struggling to stand up straight.

Joe headed for the transport terminal of his apartment, and Max sleepily stumbled after him. They went through the procedure of taking a capsule to the apartment of Freddy Soligen and emerged in due time in his quarters. Freddy stood there, his face in extreme distress, flanked by Lieutenant-Colonel Paul Warren.

Warren looked at Max Mainz coldly, but said to Joe, "Hello, Mauser, it's been a long time."

Joe said, "It has at that, Paul. May I call you Paul, Colonel? I'm an Upper myself these days—and in my time you ruined my best uniform by bleeding on it."

Warren flushed. "Certainly."

Joe said, "This is Max Mainz, my former batman, now my valued friend and assistant. I think that you both know him."

Soligen and Warren nodded to that.

Joe said to Paul Warren, "What in the hell are you doing here?"

And Warren drew himself up and said, "It would seem that Freddy has come upon the names of the top officers of a subversive organization. I am a member of the Nathan Hale Society."

"I see. And did you get them?"

"Not quite yet," Warren said. "It would seem that the bounces in caste we promised Freddy in return for this information will have to be produced before he delivers."

Joe Mauser looked at Freddy Soligen.

And Freddy said, "See here. This is gonna have to wait. I can't stay away from the telly."

That really surprised Joe Mauser. "You can't stay away from the telly. I thought you hated it."

Freddy hurried back to the set at the far side of the room. "I do," he said. "But it's the fracas between Stonewall Cogswell and Bitter Dave Langenscheidt up on the Little Big Horn Military Reservation. The Marshal's front has collapsed." He sunk down and stared at the screen.

Paul Warren, long a member of Cogswell's staff, took over. He said to Joe, whom he knew to be as

166

knowledgeable as himself, "By the way it looks, the Marshal—the Brigadier General, now—must have copped a hit early in the fracas. It's the only way I can explain what's happening." The screen was depicting field artillery shelling a rather large knoll.

Warren went on. "The Marshal has been all cut up. What remains of his regiment is on that knoll. Bitter Dave Langenscheidt is shelling it flat."

"Why in the hell doesn't Cogswell capitulate? He's obviously had it," Joe said.

Paul Warren looked at him strangely. "I suspect that he's tried to. But Bitter Dave isn't having any. He's going to finish the Marshal this time, no matter what. I suspect that he isn't honoring a white flag."

Joe stared at him in disbelief. "Any pro mercenary honors a white flag, Colonel."

And Warren said back, "They've fought four times; five, counting this fracas, and the Marshal won four of them. This time Bitter Dave has him."

"But there must be at least one or two telly pillboxes in the vicinity. They would record a white flag, and popular opinion would land hard on Bitter Dave. He'd have to accept the surrender."

"Evidently," Warren said, "the one telly pillbox that could be brought to bear is on the knoll. And it's been knocked out. I suspect it took a direct hit."

Freddy Soligen said emptily, "My boy, Sam, is up there on that hill with Stonewall Cogswell."

Chapter Seventeen

Joe looked at the telly screen.

He said, "I know that knoll. I've fought that Military Reservation three times."

Lieutenant-Colonel Paul Warren said in self-deprecation, "How well I know that you know it. It was the first time I ever met you, Joe Mauser. I was pinned down with my company there. We were both with the Marshal in that fracas. He sent you in after me. I'd copped a couple. There weren't many of my lads left unwounded by the time you got there. You carried me, or dragged me, for something like three kilometers through the enemy fire."

"Yes," Joe said musingly. "That was a long time ago. I'd almost forgotten. I think I got a bounce in rank from that, although I don't think we were on lens at the time. The Marshal was always good at taking care of his own. He didn't give a damn whether or not his men were on lens when they did something."

Max said, "What'n the hell's all this got to do with it?"

Joe looked at him and said, "We're going out to Montana. There's a little arroyo that leads up to that knoll from the rear. It's the way I got the Lieutenant-Colonel out years ago. If I have my history right, it's where one of Custer's troops were ambushed a long time ago, during his final fiasco."

Paul Warren said, "This is ridiculous." He turned to Freddy Soligen and said to him, "Your boy will have to take his chances like all the other lads in that fracas. Meanwhile, how about our business? You have the word of an Upper; if you reveal the names of the high ranking bureaucrats who head the subversives, you'll be bounced two castes."

Freddy didn't seem to care.

Joe said, "All right, Freddy, Max. Let's get going." He looked at Warren. "Well, Paul?"

Paul Warren gaped at him and said indignantly, "Do you think I'm drivel-happy? I wouldn't go into that holocaust for..."

And Joe interrupted, saying coldly, "You owe me a life, Paul Warren. I dragged you out of there something like ten years ago. You'd copped three hits. You wouldn't have lasted two hours. You're Category Military. You're an Upper and consequently consider yourself a gentleman. Are you coming?"

"Yes," Warren sighed. "You put it right forcefully, Major Mauser." He came to his feet and said, "We're in a great hurry, but do I have the time to phone my wife?"

"Why, for Zen's sake?" Freddy blurted. "Every minute counts."

Warren gave him the eye. "Because none of us are going to come back from this, Soligen."

"Go ahead," Joe said. "We've got some preliminaries. Freddy, get your lightest portable telly camera and whatever other equipment you'll need to shoot what's happening up on that knoll."

"Why?!" Freddy asked angrily. "I don't want to cast any telly. I want to get my son off that hill!"

"Because there're no cameramen on the knoll and we want to cast what's going on. Bitter Dave Langenscheidt can't get away with this curd. He's butchering those lads when they're trying to surrender. Like Paul said, he's trying to finish off Cogswell once and for all, and the funker doesn't give a damn about taking everybody else on the hill with him. Now, what do you have in the way of weapons around here, Freddy?"

Paul Warren was on the telly-phone, his face wan. He spoke softly, so the others couldn't hear what he was saying to his wife.

"Weapons?" Freddy asked. "I don't have any weapons. Oh, yeah. Sam left a 30-30 Winchester in his room. He carried it in his first fracas. In this one I think they're using Springfields."

"Get it," Joe said. "Any any ammunition for it that you can find." He turned his eyes to Max. "What are you best with, a rifle or a revolver?"

Max said, "I can't hit nothing much with a pistol."

"All right. You take the Winchester. I have my .44 Smith & Wesson. Warren has his sidearm. That'll have to do. We don't have the time to hunt up some more guns."

Freddy came back from an inner room laden down with telly equipment and the Winchester.

He said worriedly, "Joe, I'm not going to be able to cast from that hill. I'd need a lot of equipment and a crew for that. All I'll be able to do is film it, to be run later."

"All right," Joe said. "We'll film it. We're going to get that bastard Langenscheidt for this."

Paul Warren had finished his call. He turned back to them and said to Joe, "How're we going to get there? That knoll is in approximately the center of the Little Big Horn Military Reservation. And time is running out by the minute."

Joe tossed the Winchester to Max Mainz and headed for the transport terminal of Freddy's apartment. "Come on," he said, dialing for a four-seater capsule. "We'll vacuum-tube over to Billings."

They crowded into the capsule, Freddy's equipment filling most of the space. Joe dialed, even as Warren was pulling the canopy over them, and the others were buckling their belts.

"And how in the name of Zen do we get from Billings to the reservation?" Warren asked. The capsule began to sink into the bowels of the vacuum-tube transport system for the initial shot.

"We rent the fastest hovercar we can locate," Joe said.

"Wizard, but that only takes us to the edge of the reservation. Assuming we can rent horses there, it would still take us a coon's age to get to the knoll."

"We're not stopping at the edge of the reservation," Joe said grimly.

Paul Warren glowered at him. "Are you out of your mind? You can't take a vehicle onto a military reservation while a fracas is in progress. Certainly not any kind of vehicle which post-dates the year 1900."

"There's always a first time," Joe said. "If I have a very clear picture of what's going on there, we can come up behind Cogswell's position. Bitter Dave will be facing him. The hill won't be completely surrounded, since Landenscheidt doesn't have enough men for that. To completely surround it, he'd have to stretch his lads so thin that Cogswell would sally out and break through his lines. No, he's advancing on a fairly narrow front."

"Damn it, Mauser! If we're caught riding in a powered car, I'll be tossed out of Category Military and be disgraced. Soligen will be expelled from Category Communications and probably fined every share of Variable he's accumulated."

"Me, too," Max said. "I'd be tossed out of Category Military."

"Shut up, Mainz," the Lieutenant-Colonel said angrily. "What in Zen have you got to lose, you little spy?"

Max snarled, "Look who's talking. At least I don't order murders."

Paul Warren glared at him, even as the capsule suddenly surged forward. He said, "What in the hell are you talking about?"

"You guys ordered us to kill Doc Mitfield. If I'd known he was going to be any more than roughed up a

171

little, I wouldn't have gone along. But your Minuteman, Art Prager, shot the poor cloddy."

The Lieutenant Colonel's face was pale. "I don't believe it," he said. "Balt wouldn't condone anything like that, and it was Balt who arranged the whole thing."

"Only a short time ago," Joe said, "he sent five men after me in Mexico. They bombed my car, then machine-gunned it—with an illegal machinegun, by the way—and then they attempted to kill Max."

Warren said, "I'll confront Balt Haer with this, if and when I return."

"You do that," Joe told him. "If you can beat me to him."

In Billings, Warren and Soligen hurried to rent a fast car, while Joe and Max located a bookstore and bought maps of the area of Montana they were interested in, including military field maps of the reservation. Within a quarter of an hour of their arrival, they were on their way.

The edge of the Little Big Horn Military Reservation was approximately ninety kilometers to the east and included the Custer Battlefield National Monument. They made it in about half an hour. Avoiding any settlements near the border of the reservation—there were none on the reservation itself—they took off across the country.

"I still think that this is madness," Warren said. "If Bitter Dave has any cavalry scouts out, they'll spot us."

And Joe growled back, "He doesn't need to have any scouts out. He knows where Stonewall Cogswell is, and he's concentrated every man in his command before whatever entrenchments the Marshal's lads have been able to dig. When his artillery has softened them up enough, he'll go in, cavalry and all." Joe checked his field maps carefully and finally came to a halt.

"We're about three kilometers from the knoll," he

told them. "About a kilometer and a half from where the little arroyo starts. I don't dare get any closer. There's always the off chance that we'll be spotted, though I don't think it's likely. This is pretty wild country, especially since they pulled out all farmers and other former residents and gave it over to the fracases."

He had pulled up in a clump of mesquite and now the four got out. They camouflaged their vehicle, heaping fallen branches over it.

"Let's go," Freddy said in despair. "That hilltop must be like the moon by now."

"You'd be surprised how experienced sappers can dig in against a barrage," Joe said, in an attempt to console him.

But Joe wasn't that optimistic. From what little he had seen of the action, Cogswell's forces were making no answering fire at all. On the face of it, all of their field guns had been silenced. Either that, or their ammunition was gone.

They headed off, Indian style, one behind the other. Joe had shouldered Freddy Soligen's tripod, Warren had taken a gadget bag, but the telly reporter still had a considerable burden and was swearing under his breath. Joe led, keeping his right hand empty in case he needed to draw, the tripod slung over his left shoulder. Max followed, rifle loaded and ready for action. Freddy came next, and Warren brought up the rear, his holster unbuttoned. They hurried along, though not too quickly. Joe didn't want them to be out of breath if they ran into a patrol and had to shoot it out.

Joe wondered, briefly, why he seemed to be in command of their small expedition. Paul Warren, a lieutenant-colonel, out-ranked Joe, who had only been a major while he was in the Category Military. But then, he was no longer a soldier. Moreover, Pual Warren was only along under pressure.

Joe halted quickly and sank down behind a small

ridge. The others dropped, too, and Warren came crawling up. "What goes on?" he whispered.

Joe pointed and whispered back, "The beginning of the arroyo. They've got a Maxim gun there. A Maxim or a Vickers."

Paul Warren took it in. Although born an Upper, he had spent long years in the fracases with Stonewall Cogswell and wasn't unknowledgeable.

"It's a Vickers," he said, "with a four-man crew. It could keep Cogswell's whole regiment at bay."

"And Cogswell doesn't have a whole regiment any more," Joe whispered. "Well, we'll have to take it."

Warren looked over at him. "Take it? We've got one rifle and two handguns. They've got a Vickers and undoubtedly other weapons. Who do you think you are, Wild Bill Hickok?"

Joe said thoughtfully, "It would be possible to crawl around them. But suppose we did? If and when we got to the top of that damn hill, there'd be no way of coming down again, with or without any survivors. And by the sounds of that shelling, there still are survivors."

"All right," the other said. "So we take them. At least, we're behind them. They don't know we're here, and the machine-gun is pointed the other way."

Joe turned, made motions for Max to approach, and signaled to Freddy Soligen to remain where he was. Max crawled up, and Joe pointed out the machinegun nest. It had sandbags in front, but no cover behind. There was a large pile of ammunition boxes slightly to one side and behind the sandbags. The Vickers gun was equipped to hold out for some time.

Joe whispered to Max, "You go over there to the right and get yourself into as concealed a position as you can. After the first shot is fired, try to knock them off. The range isn't too bad. Here let me adjust those sights." He took the Winchester from Max's hands, squinted down at the machinegun nest, estimated expertly, and then worked quickly on the sights. "That ought to do it," he muttered, handing the gun back. "How much ammo did Freddy give you?"

"Twenty rounds."

Joe winced. "Twenty rounds? Is that all he had? Well, don't waste any."

Max began to crawl off on his belly. Perhaps he was inexperienced, but he seemed to have the instinct for it.

Joe pointed and said, "Paul, I think your best bet would be to get over there about thirty meters. What kind of gun do you have?"

".38."

"Six-inch barrel?"

"That's right."

"I've got more gun than you have, but we've still got to get to nearer range. As soon as you get over there, we'll start crawling in as quietly as possible. We'll get just as close as possible. When they finally spot us, we'll open fire. I hope the hell Max distracts them."

"Right," Warren said. "Uh, Joe."

"Yeah?"

"If you get through this and . . . I don't, will you look up my wife? We've got two kids . . ."

Joe felt an empty feeling in his belly. "I didn't know you had children, Paul."

"Well, I have."

"I wouldn't have asked you to help. If anything happens to me, Paul, will you tell Nadine Haer about it?"

"You mean, Balt's sister?"

"That's right."

"Wizard." Paul Warren began to crawl off.

It went approximately as planned . . . approximately.

Joe and Paul Warren had gotten to within twenty-five meters of the foe before one of them, as though

175

utilizing ESP, suddenly spun and spotted them. He yelled and begun madly swinging the British Vickers about.

Joe had jumped to his feet, leveled the .44, and began rapid fire. The gun was a revolver, not an automatic, and he wasn't going to have time to reload.

Things blurred then. Joe could hear Max's rifle in the background, firing away as fast as the little man could cock the lever. Joe's gun fell empty, and he dropped to the ground and felt desperately for cartridges in his jacket pocket, even as he heard the Vickers begin its chatter of death. He got three rounds into the gun, but could afford the time for no more. Max was holding their attention, drawing their fire.

He looked up. There was only one of the enemy still on his feet. Joe carefully rested the pistol on his arm and shot him. Then, still on his belly, he completely reloaded the revolver, cocked it, and cautiously came to his feet. He walked in a crouch. The gun was extended and ready for fire.

At the side of the machine-gun nest, Joe stared down and found that only one of the gunners remained alive. The man was in agony and couldn't possibly survive, especially without immediate medical care. Joe shot him through the heart to take him out of his misery.

Then he turned and made his way over to Paul Warren. Paul was still alive, but he was going fast. He looked up at Joe and said, "I owed you a life." Then he died.

Joe Mauser turned wearily and started up for the ridge of stone where Max's rifle fire had been coming from. Max was wounded. Joe pulled off his jacket and his white shirt and began ripping it into bandages.

Max said, "Zen, Joe, we really hit them, didn't we? First time I ever been in the dill in my life."

Joe worked on him quickly. Then he leaned back on

his knees and said, "Listen, Max. The closest medics are probably up on that hill. I'm going to leave you here, understand? I'll move you over to that shade, under the ridge, but then I'll have to go. I'll be back as soon as possible."

"Sure, Joe."

Chapter Eighteen

Joe Mauser put his jacket back on, picked the little man up in his arms, and carried him to the shade. Max had fainted from the pain involved in being moved, but he had revived by the time Joe returned from an expedition to get the canteens of the fallen machine-gunners. He also brought some of their army rations, though he doubted that Max was going to do any eating.

"Okay, Max," Joe said. "Hold on. We'll be back soon."

He went to one side, where Freddy Soligen could see him, and made motions for the telly reporter to come on. He took the gadget bag that Warren had been carrying earlier, including the cameraman's tripod, and led the way up the arroyo. It was narrow, winding, rocky, and difficult to ascend. Before them, the shelling seemed to have lessened considerably in intensity. Damn it, was Bitter Dave preparing for the assault?

"I hope the hell we make it in time, after all this," Joe muttered. Freddy merely groaned, saving his breath the better to tote his heavy equipment.

The final score of meters were the steepest and both were panting when they reached the summit. A voice rang out, "Halt!" And then, registering astonishment, "Who in the hell are you?"

"Friends," Joe answered. Both Joe and Freddy were in civilian clothes, and both were carrying telly camera equipment, so Joe wasn't particularly afraid of being shot.

"Well, get the hell out of here, before you get your asses shot off."

Instead, they hurried forward, bent double. Before

jumping down into the entrenchments, Joe shot a quick look about the knoll. It was a shambles. Ruined equipment, including two knocked out field guns and several wagons, was everywhere. The horses that had originally drawn the wagons were dead and stretched out on the ground. Exposed to the sun, they already stank.

There were only two men in this section of the trench; obviously, the marshal didn't expect attack from this point. Both of the men were dirty and unshaven and their clothes were a mess. Both carried rifles, although one of them was a captain. His name was Bowles.

The captain stared at Joe. "Why, you're Major Joe Mauser. Where the hell'd you come from?" he asked.

"By a path I know about from an earlier fracas. What's the situation, Captain?"

"You've been kicked out of Category Military. You're not allowed on a reservation during a fracas."

"What's the situation?" Joe asked nonetheless.

"Everything's pickled. Only a few of us made it here to this summit. The general took a freak hit early in the action and was put out of the running."

"That's what Warren thought happened," Joe muttered. "Go on."

"We tried to capitulate, but Bitter Joe wasn't having any. Only a handful of us got to this point. We dug in. He brought up all of his field artillery and has been shelling us ever since. We keep digging further in, but we're still taking casualties, although the fire's falling off."

"Where's the Marshal?" Joe said.

"This way," The captain led, leaving his one private behind to continue to watch the area that had been thought impassable, but which Joe and Freddy had proved otherwise.

Freddy called after him, "Do you know a Rank Private named Sam Soligen?"

"I don't think so," Bowles said, turning down a traverse trench. There were wounded stretched out on army blankets on the floor of the trench and the captain, Joe, and Freddy had to wind in and out among them. Joe could see that some of them had already died. He wondered where they were putting the rest of the already dead. They certainly didn't have the time for burial squads, nor could they afford to expose themselves.

"How many officers do you have left?" he asked Bowles.

"Three, including me. Another captain and a lieutenant. Both have copped one, but are still on their feet."

They reached a larger trench and came to a dugout. They entered and found an improvised field hospital. A single kerosene mantle lamp lit it. The floor was covered with wounded men. There was an improvised operating table composed of several wooden ammunition boxes that had once held artillery shells. A single doctor, his once white coat smeared with blood, worked wearily with two medics. The doctor had obviously been at it for more hours than he could remember.

"Where's the general?" Joe asked him.

"Over in the corner. He comes and goes in and out of delirium."

A shell broke above the dugout and dirt sifted down from the ceiling.

Joe, followed by Captain Bowles, went over to the army cot Stonewall Cogswell was lying on. It was the only cot in the dugout. The former Field Marshal looked lucid, though he seemed to be in pain. He was breathing deeply.

He looked up at Joe and recognized him. "Mauser?" he asked. "Take over, Mauser. Get my lads out of this death trap." Then his eyes glazed and he began muttering meaninglessly. He ordered General Jack Alshuler to take his heavy cavalry around the enemy's flank.

Meanwhile, Freddy was anxiously questioning the doctor, "Sam Soligen, Rank Private. You know anything about him?"

The doctor motioned wearily with his head. "He's over there, against that wall. Battle fatigue. They used to call it shell-shock. He'll be all right, when and if we can get him back to a hospital."

Freddy hurried over, letting the doctor go back to his job of patching up bodies.

Joe said to Bowles, "Let's give this situation a look." Joe headed back for the entrance to the dugout. "Let's meet the other officers," he said. "The shelling seems to have fallen off considerably."

In the trench outside they began to run into Rank Privates and Non-coms. Some were at work digging more dugouts; some were repairing sections of the entrenchments that had been caved in by the shellfire.

Bowles explained. "We're in deep enough that it takes a direct hit or a burst of shrapnel immediately overhead to inflict any casualties."

"But it's just a matter of time," Joe growled.

They came up on a trench which overlooked the valley below. In it were a captain and a lieutenant, both bandaged, using binoculars. In the far distance, Joe Mauser could make out Bitter Dave's forces, even with the naked eye.

"Hank, Chris," Bowles said, summoning the two in the trench.

They turned. Bowles said, "Major Joe Mauser, this is Captain Fordham and Lieutenant Vance."

The two stared at Joe. There wasn't a man in Category Military, certainly not an officer, who didn't know the Joe Mauser story. It was commonly thought that Major Mauser had taken a raw deal from the Category Military Department.

Captain Bowles cleared his throat and said, "General Cogswell has just turned the command over to Major Mauser."

Captain Fordham turned his stare to Bowles. "Are you drivel-happy? Mauser isn't even an officer any more. He's not even in Category Military. It's illegal for him to even be on the Military Reservation with a fracas going on."

"We'll worry about that after we get down off this hill," Joe told him flatly. "Let me have your glasses, captain."

Fordham handed over his binoculars.

Joe Mauser looked out over the terrain for long time. Finally, he brought them down and turned to the three worn-out infantry officers.

He said, "The reason the barrage has fallen off is because Bitter Dave has run short of shells. But I can make out supply wagons coming up. But there's something worse than that. He's also bringing up two heavy mortars—real heavies. When he gets them into firing position, the top of this hill won't last an hour. We've got to pull out soon."

"Pull out?" Chris Vance asked bitterly. "If we could pull out don't you think we would have done it yesterday? See those white flags?" He pointed out two white flags. "We can't even surrender."

Joe said, "There's a path of sorts, leading down an arroyo to your rear. Have your men throw away their guns, their grenades, and every other weapon they might have on hand. Have them improvise as many stretchers as they can. We'll head down the hill. The

182

walking wounded and those who haven't copped one will carry or support those badly hit. Get to it. If Bitter Dave gets his new supply of shells up, we've had it."

"Why throw away our guns?" Fordham said, scowling with resentment.

"Because there's not enough of you still operative to make any difference, anyway. Sooner or later, your retreating column will run into some of Bitter Dave's lads. As soon as he discovers the hill is short of men, he'll send out cavalry patrols to locate you. The minute you see even one of Langenscheidt's lads, everybody will throw up his arms in surrender."

"They'd mow us down," Bowles said. "They won't let us surrender. Like Chris here pointed out, they're not observing our white flags."

"No, they won't," Joe said, exuding more confidence than he felt. "Those men down there are mercenaries. Bitter Dave is so enraged at Stonewall that he's drivel-happy, but no professional mercenary is going to cut down a column of unarmed men. They might find themselves in a similar pickled situation a month from now. Get to it, men."

The three officers left to obey his orders.

Freddy Soligen came up, lugging his equipment. He said, "The doc says Sam will be all right, if we can get out of here. He'll never be able to fight in another fracas, which is okay as far as I'm concerned. What do I do now, Joe?"

"Get to work. Get those white flags on film. Get all those wounded lads laying in the bottom of the trenches, and get the men throwing away their guns. Try to get some pathos into it. Just don't film me."

"Wizard," Freddy said. He began to set up his tripod.

Joe said, "One more thing, Freddy. If we pull this off we'll throw the book at Langenscheidt. And you'll have pulled off the biggest beat in the history of Category

Communications, Branch Fracas News. Every buff in the country will be shouting your praises. You'll get your two bounces in caste."

Freddy looked at him and said, "The only thing that counts at all is getting Sam off this damned hill before the shelling starts again."

Lieutenant Chris Vance came up. He looked haggard. "We're short of stretchers, Major. How about using rifles for stretcher poles? We have some tents in one of the wagons. We could cut them up and improvise with the canvas."

Joe shook his head. "No. When we go off this hill, there won't be a weapon on us. We give them no excuse to fire." He brought his own pistol from his belt and threw it to one side. "Not even sidearms, Lieutenant." He thought about the problem. "As a suggestion, chop up those wagons above and make stretcher poles out of the wood."

"Yes, sir," Vance said.

Joe said to Freddy, "When we leave, abandon your equipment. Take only the film you've exposed."

"Are you kidding? It's worth..."

"You'll be helping to carry a stretcher, Freddy. Sam will be on it."

Joe Mauser took the glasses up again and searched out Bitter Dave's position. He didn't like the speed at which the shell bearing wagons and the mortars were coming up. But there was nothing he could do about that.

He retraced the route to the improvised field hospital in the dugout. The shelling had stopped completely. At least that was a blessing. Everywhere, the men were putting together stretchers and moving the more desperately wounded onto them.

Joe went into the dugout. The doctor, though standing, was standing over his operating table, his

184

head on his arms. The two medics were sitting on the floor, for lack of somewhere else to sit. They were obviously as far gone as their chief.

Joe said, "All right, let's start moving out. We've got to get going down that hill before they open up again. If they catch us in the open we're sitting ducks."

The doctor raised his head in absolute weariness.

Joe said, "There's a badly wounded man down below. We had to shoot our way up the arroyo. Bring your kit, and you and I will go out in the lead."

"All right."

Joe went over to where Stonewall Cogswell was stretched out on his army cot. He looked down at the man he had fought under a dozen times, and pulled back the blanket over him for a quick check. The right leg was shattered. There wasn't a chance that it could ever be saved. The former Marshal would be lucky if he got out alive.

Joe looked at one of the medics and said, "Give me a hand. We'll carry the whole cot."

Then he looked down at Stonewall Cogswell. Meaninglessly, he said, "All right, Stonewall, we'll go across the river and into the trees."

It was a tortuous descent, but they made it.

At the foot, Joe said to the stumbling doctor, "Over here." Joe led the way to where he had left Max. Freddy brought up the rear, bearing his rolls of telly film.

Joe stared down at Max Mainz. He shook his head and closed his eyes in pain and said, "Sorry, Max. Sorry."

He turned back to Freddy Soligen and said, "We've got to get out of here; we've got to get back to the car and off the reservation."

"How about Sam?"

"He's better off with the Doc than he would be with us. Come on, Freddy. We've done all we could."

Aftermath

The general presiding at the court martial said, "Joseph Mauser, former Category Military, former Rank Major, Lower-Upper. You have heard the charges. If found guilty by law you must be sentenced to lifelong imprisonment. Are the charges correct?"

Joe Mauser said respectfully, "Sir, I plead the Fifth Amendment."

The five members of the court martial, including the general, looked at him blankly.

"The what?" the general said.

"Sir, when the Revised Constitution was compiled, the Bill of Rights was allowed to remain, although they are seldom, if ever, invoked these days. More sweeping changes largely cover the territory they once did. However, the Fifth Amendment is still in the Revised Constitution, and I refuse to testify on the grounds that it might incriminate me."

The general looked at the colonel who was handling the prosecution. The colonel had belonged to the Category Law before he switched to Category Military.

He cleared his throat and said, "He is correct, Sir." He looked at Joe Mauser. "But how would you know? Where did you ever read law? You were a mercenary soldier."

Joe said with a shrug, "In hospital beds, when there was nothing else to read, and after I'd copped one. In my day, I've copped many a one."

The general presiding shook his head, looked down at the papers before him, and said, "Brigadier Hillary Cogswell..."

Joe Mauser, who had reseated himself, looked up, a

touch of a wry smile on his mouth. He had never heard Cogswell's first name before. For fifteen years, during which time he had fought with the former marshal on one side or the other, it had been *Stonewall* Cogswell, because of his victories and his dedication to the study of the campaigns of the Civil War hero of the South.

The presiding general was going on, ". . . Category Military, Rank Brigadier General, Low-Upper." The general looked down at Stonewall Cogswell, who was now standing on crutches, one of his arms still in a sling. "As an Upper caste member, General, it is, of course, not necessary for you to testify under oath."

Noblesse oblige, Joe thought cynically. An Upper didn't lie. A Middle, and especially a Lower, testified under oath and were subject to being brought up for perjury. But not an Upper.

The presiding general said respectfully, "Would you give your testimony of the events on the hill during your fracas with General Langenscheidt?"

Stonewall Cogswell looked over at the defense table and at Joe Mauser. Then Cogswell's eyes came back to the general presiding. He said, "I was unconscious, as a result of my wounds. I might add, in the way of a character reference that former Major Joseph Mauser has been an acquaintance for at least a decade and a half. I have been in the dill with him more than once. I have always found him the epitome of a capable officer and a most gallant one."

The prosecutor groaned. This was being televised. The former Marshal Cogswell was possibly the most celebrated of all fracas commanding officers. In his time, he had won more battles than Napoleon. Besides that, the country was up in arms against what had transpired on the hill in Langenscheidt's attempt to finish him. And the general's wounds were obvious. He had lost his leg.

The general presiding said courteously, "Thank you General Cogswell."

He looked down at the papers before him. "Fredric Soligen, Category Communications, Subdivision Telly, Branch Fracas News, Low-Middle. Citizen Soligen, will you give your testimony?"

The feisty cameraman came to his feet belligerently, took the oath, and said, "I don't know what in Zen this is all about. Joe got kicked out of the Category Military and dint know what to do with his time. He was like an old warhorse with nothing to do. So I kind of took mercy on him. I gave him a job as an assistant..."

"Just a moment," the prosecutor said sharply, "Are you saying that the former Major Mauser has switched categories to Category Communications?"

"Well, no. Not yet. What we wanted to do was get him a good send off, something impressive so he'd get a good rank in Telly, Branch Fracas News. With his experience, he was a natural. Nobody's had more experience in the fracases than Joe Mauser." Freddy apologetically looked over at Stonewall Cogswell. "Except the Marshal, of course."

The presiding general said, "All right, all right. Go on, Citizen Soligen."

"Well, anyway, Joe had fought on that reservation before. He knew the terrain. He'd even been on that knoll where the Marshal was pinned down. He figured if we could get up there—the telly pillbox had been knocked out—we'd have a telly-beat. It wasn't being covered from the Marshal's side."

"The general's side," the prosecutor said impatiently.

Freddy Soligen looked at him. "Ye, sir," he said. "But I'll always think of him as Field Marshal Stonewall Cogswell, and so will most fracas buffs." Freddy knew damn well he was on lens and that every fracas fan in the United States of the Americas was taking this in.

Every knowledgeable buff in the country was lined up on the side of the Marshal and the perennially unlucky Joe Mauser. Freddy was losing no points.

"Go on," the presiding general said.

Freddy said, "It was all Joe's idea to get the coverage for the fracas-buffs." Freddy looked noble. "That's the job of Telly, Branch Fracas News. Getting the coverage for the fans. It's a pretty inspiring way of making a living."

"Good Jumping Zen," the prosecutor blurted out.

"That will be all, Colonel," the presiding general said sharply. "Go on, Citizen Soligen."

"Well, Joe knew about this little path up an arroyo, and he figured we could get up there and. . . ."

"Was he armed?" the prosecutor interrupted.

Freddy looked at him blankly. "Armed? He was all loaded down with my equipment. You think a telly reporter just carries a camera with him? He's gotta have all sorts of special lenses and a tripod and all that sort of thing. It's not as easy a job as you think, Colonel."

"All right, continue. What happened when you got to that Vickers gun emplacement with four of General Langenscheidt's men manning it?"

Freddy stared at him. "What'd you think happened? Lieutenant Colonel Warren, who was usually a member of the Marshal's staff, and Rank Private Max Mainz, a lad who had fought under the Marshal before, took them from behind. Their gun was pointed the opposite way. They weren't expecting anybody to come up from the rear."

The prosecutor asked sharply, "And the former Major Mauser didn't participate?"

Freddy was still looking at him with disbelief. "How could he? He was carrying all this here equipment of mine."

The presiding general looked at Stonewall Cogswell.

The former marshal said, "Lieutenant Colonel Paul Warren has been on my staff in many a fracas. He was a gallant officer. Knowing that my situation had pickled and that I was in the dill, he would have given his life, and did, to come to my aid."

The prosecutor groaned inwardly again and said aloud to Freddy Soligen, "All right, all right, go on."

"What else is there? We went on up and got to the knoll, and me and Joe Mauser got some good coverage. And then we all got out of there before old Bitter Dave could come up with his heavy mortars."

"And did former Major Mauser give military advice to Marshal Cogswell or his surviving officers?"

Freddy said plaintively, "He didn't have to. They could all see the way we'd come up. And the Marshal, like he said, had already passed out."

The prosecuting colonel rolled his eyes upward. He knew perfectly well that the little man was lying. So did everybody else. He said, "Next witness."

The next three witnesses were Captains Bowles and Fordham and Lieutenant Vance. They lied like gentlemen.

At the end, the prosecutor brought Joe to his feet again. He said, "Joseph Mauser, all testimony has indicated your innocence of the charges. Why, then, should it be necessary for you to plead the Fifth?"

Joe said evenly, "I plead the Fifth Amendement to that question and refuse to answer on the grounds that it might incriminate me."

The prosecutor sighed and turned to the general presiding. "The case rests," he said in resignation.

The general looked at the other four members of the court. He said, "Gentlemen, is there any necessity for us to leave the bench to deliberate?"

The colonel to his left growled, "I believe he's guilty

as charged, damn it. However, there is no evidence. I vote, not guilty."

The other three said:

"Not guilty."

"Not guilty."

"Not guilty."

Two of them, in their time, had participated with Joe in the fracases. The others knew him by reputation. Joe's reputation in the Category Military couldn't be higher.

"The case against Joseph Mauser is dismissed."

After the others had filed out and Joe had thanked Cogswell, Soligen and the others, a court attendant approached him and said, "Major Mauser, a representative of the North American Bureau of Investigation wishes to speak with you. He is in the adjoining office."

Joe thanked him and made his way to the indicated room. As he opened the door he noted that the room was soundproofed. Frank Hodgson, Nadine Haer, and Philip Holland were there.

Joe said, "Case dismissed."

The three of them sighed with relief.

Hodgson said, "And Soligen?"

"Wild horses couldn't drag information about the organization out of him. However, behind the scenes it wouldn't hurt to have he and his son bounced up to High-Middle."

"We'll see what we can do," Holland said.

Frank Hodgson took a deep breath and looked from one of them to the other. He said, "We have found it impossible to convert any reasonable number of either Middles or Lowers. We're stymied in our efforts to overthrow People's Capitalism. The organization is just going to have to continue as best it can until we can come up with some gimmick to get the country moving.

191

Are all of you still in?"

Phil Holland chuckled sardonically and didn't bother to answer.

"Nadine said, "Yes."

And Joe Mauser said, "I'm still in."